ECO
CRASH

CHANGINGUN!VERSE

Also available in this series:
SS WORLD

ECO

CRASH

Terrance Dicks
Piccadilly Press • London

CHANGINGUN!VERSE

Printed and bound by WBC, Bridgend,
for the publishers Piccadilly Press Ltd,
5 Castle Road, London NW1 8PR

A catalogue record for this book is available from
the British Library

ISBNs: 1 85340 507 8 (trade paperback)
1 85340 512 4 (hardback)

1 3 5 7 9 10 8 6 4 2

Terrance Dicks lives in North London. He has written many books
for Piccadilly Press including THE UNEXPLAINED series, the
CHRONICLES OF A COMPUTER GAME ADDICT series, the HARVEY series
and THE GOOD, THE BAD AND THE GHASTLY series.

Design by Judith Robertson
Cover design by Mandy Sherliker

PROLOGUE

TOM WAS under water, struggling for breath . . .

Looking up he could see dull grey light, not too far overhead.

He stretched up his arms and kicked frantically. He wasn't the best swimmer in the world and he was desperate to reach the surface before he drowned.

Suddenly his head shot out of the water and he gasped in a lungful of acrid, choking air.

Treading water, he looked around him. He was in a patch of grimy, turbulent water over the surface of which drifted yellow, sulphurous fog. Overhead, lightning flashed in the murky skies, and there was a steady rumble of thunder.

But where was Sarah?

'Sarah!' he yelled. 'Sarah, where are you?'

Looking around, Tom saw a dark mass rising out of the water. Whatever it was it looked solid and he swam towards it.

The dark shape turned out to be a pile of shattered stonework. He climbed on to the rubble and looked around.

'Sarah!' Tom shouted again as he clung to the flooded rubble. 'Sarah, where are you?'

He tried to peer through the choking mists and gain his bearings in this strange, hostile landscape.

Maybe she didn't make it to the surface, he thought. Maybe she drowned . . .

'Sarah!' he called again.

'It's all right, Tom,' called a voice behind him. 'I'm here!'

Turning, Tom saw a bedraggled Sarah climbing over the rubble towards him. He grinned in relief. He needn't have worried about Sarah. She could look after herself just as well as he could – probably better.

Given the chance, Tom was a couch potato, spending hours watching his beloved old-fashioned films.

Sarah was a keen athlete, a daily jogger – and an excellent swimmer. Obviously she'd seen the pile of rubble when she surfaced, just as he had, and had reached it before him.

She clambered on to the same chunk of rubble and crouched down beside him. 'Are you all right, Tom?'

'Apart from being half-drowned, lost and terrified, you mean?' He looked round and shuddered. 'What a terrible place.'

'You're telling me. We've done it this time – or the

6

transmat has. Where on earth are we? And what's happened here?'

Tom shrugged. 'Something pretty drastic. Nuclear war, maybe? Civilisation in ruins, like in *Planet of the Apes*?'

'Like what?'

'It's a movie. There's a terrible nuclear war, mankind is almost wiped out and the apes take over. The surviving humans become their slaves.'

'Never mind your old movies, Tom,' said Sarah impatiently. 'We need to find out where we are, and what's happened.'

Tom studied their gloomy surroundings, and the little island of rubble where they sat.

'Hang on a minute,' he said. 'Maybe my old movie idea's not so far out after all!'

'What do you mean?'

'Well, just look at what we're sitting on.'

They both looked down. They were sitting on a big rounded piece of masonry like a section of a giant stone log. There were ridges running along the sides.

Sarah looked at Tom as if he were mad. 'What about it?'

'This astronaut . . .'

'What astronaut?'

'The one in the *Planet of the Apes* movie. At first he thinks he's on an alien planet. But at the end of the movie he finds a huge statue lying in the sands.'

'Well, what about it?'

'It's the Statue of Liberty! So, if my theory is correct . . .'

'What theory?'

'Come with me!'

Tom led the way towards the centre of the pile of rubble. Suddenly he stopped and pointed downwards. 'Look!'

Looking up at them was the face of a lion.

Tom scrambled onwards and then stopped again. 'You see?'

The jagged stump of a column rose from the centre of the pile of rubble. Close beside it there lay the shattered remnants of a statue. The body was broken into several pieces, but the face with its eyepatch stared upwards at the murky skies.

'It's not the Statue of Liberty,' said Tom, 'but you see what I mean?' He sighed. 'Poor old Nelson!'

'We're still in Trafalgar Square!' said Sarah slowly. 'In a flooded, ruined London.'

It was a terrifying thought, and for a moment Sarah was stunned. They'd survived so many dangers – and now this.

'Now what?' she said despairingly. 'What are we going to do? No food, no shelter. We could die here.'

Tom looked around the gloomy scene.

Not that you could see much. Just darkness and swirling mists, illuminated by the occasional flash of lightning.

'Well, unless it's like this all the time here, it seems to be night-time,' he said. 'I think we'd better just wait here till dawn. With any luck it'll clear up a bit.'

'All right,' said Sarah dully.

Tom put his arm round her consolingly, and they sat huddled together in the darkness.

However did we wind up here? thought Tom. All we wanted to do is get home . . .

PARALLEL WORLDS

TOM AND Sarah's extraordinary adventures had begun on Earth in the year 2015. They'd grown up in a happy, prosperous, pollution-free world, thanks largely to the invention of the instantaneous matter transmission system – transmat for short.

You got into a transmat booth, dialled the correct coordinates – and dematerialised. Seconds later you reappeared – in a transmat booth at your chosen destination, in another city or even another country.

Tom and Sarah Martin were first cousins – their fathers were brothers and their mothers were sisters. When Sarah's mother and father had been killed in one of the last plane crashes, Tom's parents had taken her in. The two had been brought up together as brother and sister.

They'd been making a routine transmat journey from New York to London when things had gone terribly wrong.

Because of a freak electrical storm, transmat had malfunctioned, sending them not to the wrong place but to the wrong dimension.

They had arrived in Trafalgar Square in an alternative world where the Nazis had won World War Two, and the statue on the column in Trafalgar Square wasn't Horatio Nelson but Adolf Hitler.

After a number of terrifying and dangerous adventures in a London ruled by the ruthless Nazi SS, they'd finally managed to escape.

The way they'd left this parallel universe had been even more extraordinary than their arrival.

They'd run into their alternative selves, the Tom and Sarah of this other world. For some reason it wasn't possible for two Toms and two Sarahs to exist side by side in the same dimension.

Transmat, to which they still seemed to be mysteriously linked, had snatched them away from the SS world. They'd found themselves sitting on a bench in an apparently normal Trafalgar Square.

They'd thought the adventure was over, that they were safely back home.

They were wrong.

Now, wet, miserable and dazed, huddled next to Sarah on the little island of rubble, Tom tried to piece together in his memory the extraordinary sequence of events that had followed.

It was only a matter of minutes after arriving in

Trafalgar Square that things had started going wrong . . . when Tom and Sarah realised that it was Napoleon and not Nelson on top of 'Nelson's' Column . . . and that someone had overheard them speaking English when it was illegal not to speak French in the police state of the Napoleonic World . . . and that once again they were on the run from armed police. They seemed to be reliving the nightmare of the SS World over again: trapped, desperately trying to avoid capture and find a way of escape – but before they had had any chance to adjust to their latest predicament, they had – literally – run into the other-world Tom and Sarah, and Trafalgar Square had faded away . . .

. . . and Tom and Sarah had found themselves under water, struggling for breath . . .

CHAPTER TWO

RUINED CITY

AND NOW here they were, on an island of rubble in a wrecked and flooded Trafalgar Square.

In an incredibly short space of time they'd escaped the dangers of the Nazi world, passed briefly through the Napoleonic one, and ended up here, in yet another alternative universe.

In a world where things had obviously gone horribly wrong.

Half-dozing, Tom felt Sarah's bony elbow jab him in the ribs.

'Wake up, Tom, it's starting to get light.'

Tom yawned and stretched. He stood up and looked around him. The mists were slowly beginning to clear and a fitful sun gleamed between lowering black clouds.

'Terrific,' he said. 'Now we can *see* what a ghastly place we're in!'

'Well, we can't just sit here, we'll starve to death. We've

got to get off here and find food and shelter.'

Tom was relieved to hear that Sarah sounded more like her old self. Her practical mind had already started to adjust to the disaster. Now she was thinking of ways to deal with it.

He looked at the murky water lapping around the little island. 'The only way off here is to swim,' he pointed out.

'Then we'll swim!'

'Yes, but where to and how far?' objected Tom. 'We don't know how much of London is flooded. We could just go on swimming until we drown!'

'Better than sitting here till we starve!' said Sarah. 'If we're above water here, there's bound to be other places above water too.' She scrambled to the highest point of the pile of rubble and Tom followed her.

Sarah looked around. Below them, the mists drifted apart briefly.

'Over that way there doesn't seem to be anything but water. I reckon that must be south – the land slopes down towards the Thames, so the flooding would be worse in that direction. Probably all the Thames estuary is under water.' She swung round. 'If that's south, this is north – and that way the land climbs pretty steeply upwards. So, if we swim north we stand a better chance of finding dry land – high ground that the flood waters haven't reached. And North London's where we happen to live – in our own world, anyway.'

'Suppose we meet ourselves in this world?'

'We'll get bounced to yet another alternative universe, I suppose.'

'Do we want to take that chance?'

Sarah shrugged. 'Why not? It's almost bound to be better than this one.'

'It's a heck of a risk,' grumbled Tom. 'Still, what have we got to lose?'

'Look!' said Sarah suddenly.

The drifting mists had cleared once more, revealing a pile of jagged ruins.

'I bet that's what's left of the National Gallery!'

'I hope you're right,' said Tom, 'and that there's dry land beyond it. Well, back to the water!'

'At least it's not too cold,' said Sarah.

Tom realised that she was right. The air around them was warm and humid. Even the water itself hadn't really been all that cold.

'No it's amazingly warm,' he said.

'That could be a clue.'

'A clue to what?'

'To what's happened,' said Sarah. 'Come on, let's get moving.'

They scrambled down to the edge of the island of rubble and launched themselves into the water.

Sarah sped ahead in a rapid crawl, while Tom puffed behind her in a laboured breaststroke.

Fortunately for him the swim wasn't a long one. Before long they were climbing out of the water and up a flight of broken steps that led to the ruins of the National Gallery.

Tom went to the edge of the steps and peered up what had once been Charing Cross Road.

'What can you see?' asked Sarah.

'More of the same,' said Tom gloomily. 'Water, mud and ruins. We might just as well have stayed on the island.' Overcome by sudden despair, he sat down on the steps, elbows on his knees and his head in his hands.

Sarah looked anxiously at him. 'Come on, Tom, snap out of it.'

'We went through all the dangers of that Nazi world,' said Tom bitterly, 'we managed to survive and we even got away. I thought we were home, thought I'd see Mum and Dad again – my real mum and dad. Then it turned out we were in that weird French world – and if that wasn't bad enough, we get bounced from there to this hell-hole! It's just not fair!'

'"Whoever said life was going to be fair, boy?"' said Sarah. It was one of Tom's father's favourite sayings.

Tom gave a reluctant grin. 'Yeah, you're right. We're here because we're here and it's no use moaning about it. We must decide what to do next.'

'Obvious,' said Sarah. 'When the going gets tough, the tough go shopping!'

Tom stared at her. 'Shopping?'

'Well, just look at us!'

'What about us?'

'These clothes, for a start.'

They were still wearing the clothes they'd acquired in the SS world.

Tom had a shirt, slacks and tunic in some soft grey material, and Sarah wore a bedraggled blue velvet dress.

Tom looked down at his thin and soggy garments. 'I see what you mean. We're not really equipped for these conditions, are we? We need tougher clothing, food supplies, maybe even weapons.'

Sarah frowned. 'Why weapons?'

'We don't know what the animals are like on this version of Earth. Or the people either, come to that.'

Sarah, a life-long pacifist, shook her head. 'I don't like the idea of weapons.'

'I don't like the idea of dying!' said Tom. 'Look, forget about weapons for the moment. We're certainly going to need food, and some more practical clothes.'

Sarah thought for a moment. 'We'll go to Oxford Street,' she said. 'It's not far away and there are lots of big department stores there. They'll have everything we need under one roof.'

'If they're not ruined or flooded – and if there's anything left,' said Tom. 'We don't know how long ago this catastrophe happened.'

'Well, let's go and look,' said Sarah practically.

They began the long struggle up Charing Cross Road.

Close to the flooded square the road was awash with water and they had to splash their way through it. Soon the water gave way to thick mud, which wasn't much of an improvement.

It began to rain, a sudden torrential downpour. Since they were already soaked to the skin the rain didn't bother them too much. But it was exhausting having to force their way through. It came down in what felt like solid sheets of water. You almost had to push your way through it. It was accompanied by a terrifying lightning storm.

A jagged bolt of lightning struck the roof of a nearby building and huge chunks of rubble crashed down close to their heads.

'Probably what happened to poor old Nelson!' Tom shuddered, jumping back.

The rainstorm ended as suddenly as it had begun. A fierce sun came out somewhere above the murky clouds. They couldn't see it, but its heat raised clouds of steam from their wet clothes, and from the ruined buildings around them.

'Whatever's happened here, it hasn't done much for the climate,' said Tom. 'Drowned and sunburned all on the same day!'

'I think climate's what it's all about,' said Sarah.

'How do you mean?'

'Tell you later,' said Sarah. 'I'm still working it out.'

They trudged on their way.

Tom was wondering what they were going to find.

What terrible catastrophe had altered the climate and reduced London to this state?

Meteorites?

Alien invasion?

20

Nuclear war?

And how were they going to survive in this terrible world?

CHAPTER THREE

THE BIG STORE

IT WASN'T an easy journey. The road was swamped with mud and rubble. The windows of shops and offices were smashed in and their interiors a muddy ruin.

The pavement under their feet was broken and uneven, but at least it wasn't flooded. They could walk rather than swim.

'I was right, wasn't I?' said Sarah. 'The flood waters don't reach very far north beyond Trafalgar Square.'

'You're right just for the moment,' said Tom. 'Luckily for us. But don't assume it's permanent.'

'What do you mean?'

'What do you think did all this damage? And this mud's still wet. Look!' Tom pointed to a kind of high-water mark along the walls of the ruined building they were passing. 'I reckon the flood water's been right up here and gone down. Which means it might come back up again!'

Sarah looked round and shuddered. 'The sooner we get

on to some really high ground the better.' She looked at Tom. 'We must make some kind of plan.'

'We will,' said Tom. 'But first of all we must make sure we can manage to stay alive. Problems here are a bit more basic than on the SS World.'

Sarah nodded. 'This is simpler, I suppose. We had a hostile society to deal with there. Here there's just – nothing.'

Tom tried to cheer her up. 'Maybe it's a local catastrophe. We don't know what happened in other parts of the country. Or in other parts of the world, come to that.'

Sarah gave him a sceptical look. 'You think they're all alive and well in Tunbridge Wells or somewhere?'

'Why not?'

Sarah looked up at the dark, sultry skies. 'All this has a nasty global feel to me. I wouldn't mind betting the entire planet is affected. The weather's changed, the whole climate feels different.'

'So what caused it?' asked Tom. 'And what happened to everyone?' He repeated some of the ideas that had been passing through his mind. 'In the old science-fiction movies it was nuclear war, or alien invasion, or Earth struck by giant meteorites . . .'

'I think we caused it,' said Sarah.

'Us?'

'Well, not us personally, but mankind, humanity. It very nearly happened on our world, you know.'

'It did?'

'Have you ever heard of global warming?'

Tom nodded. 'Just about. Weren't people worrying about it in the last part of the twentieth century?'

'That's right,' said Sarah. 'They very nearly started worrying too late.'

'How do you mean?'

'They were putting so much pollution, and so many harmful chemical emissions into the atmosphere that the protective ozone layer round the world was weakened. The whole planet started warming up. Scientists predicted that if it went on the polar icecaps would melt – which would mean massive flooding and probably change weather patterns as well.'

'Which is what we've seen here,' said Tom slowly.

'That's right,' said Sarah. 'Exactly what we've seen here.'

They had reached the top of Charing Cross Road by now, and were turning left into the equally desolate Oxford Street.

Tom looked up at the gloomy skies. 'So all this devastation is down to this – global warming?'

'It could be.'

'So why didn't it happen in our world? People came to their senses in time, right?'

Sarah nodded. 'All over the world governments passed laws to cut down on pollution. And of course, what really saved us was the invention of transmat. That got rid of most of the pollution at one go.'

'So here, in this parallel world, maybe they didn't come to their senses?'

'That's right,' said Sarah grimly. 'And maybe they didn't invent transmat either!'

They looked at each other in sudden dismay.

Their best hope of getting back to their own universe was eventually to find some scientists who understood transmat well enough to send them there.

And if transmat hadn't even been invented . . .

'That means we'll never get away from here,' said Tom.

'Not unless we do manage to get to our house and meet our this-world selves,' said Sarah. 'And for all we know they were drowned years ago.'

'No!' said Tom suddenly.

'No what?'

'No to our arriving in a world that never invented transmat,' said Tom. 'I don't quite know why, but I'm sure that if that was the case we just wouldn't be here.'

'Why not?'

'Because we're still linked to transmat in some way. I don't think it could send us to a world where it didn't exist.'

'We didn't see a transmat station in that Napoleonic World.'

'Doesn't mean that there wasn't one somewhere around, though, does it?' argued Tom. 'It was probably reserved for government big-wigs, like on the SS World.'

Sarah still wasn't convinced. 'If they've got transmat

here, why did all this flooding and climate change happen? Transmat would have helped them to end the pollution and the gas emissions.'

Tom held obstinately to his theory – maybe because it was the only one that offered them any hope. 'Perhaps they didn't quite perfect transmat here,' he said. 'Or maybe they invented it too late. Something went wrong, obviously. All the same, somewhere, somehow in this messed-up world – transmat exists!'

'I hope you're right!' said Sarah.

'I'd better be, hadn't I?' said Tom.

They saw a big department store just ahead on the right. Its massive square shape, like some ancient fortress, seemed to have survived the storms and the floods almost unharmed.

As they got closer however, they saw that the big display windows had been smashed in. The doors hung open as well.

'Doubt if there'll be anything much worth having left by now,' said Tom. 'Still we'd better take a look.'

Cautiously they moved through the gaping main doors. The light from the street illuminated the area around the doorway. Beyond that there stretched a huge cave of shadowy darkness.

Tom shook his head in despair. 'Even if there is anything useful we're never going to be able to find it!'

'Hang on,' said Sarah. 'I think I know this place. As I remember, the food section was somewhere on the left. We might as well start there. Come on!'

They moved along shadowy aisles between shattered display cases, the light growing dimmer all the time.

'What we need is a nice big torch,' muttered Tom.

'In full working order, complete with batteries, I suppose. You don't ask for much!'

'No harm in hoping! Aha, what's this?'

Tom went over to a pile of assorted objects to his left and rummaged amongst them.

'What have you got?' asked Sarah.

Tom examined his finds. 'A toaster and an electric food mixer, I think.'

'Very useful,' said Sarah.

Tossing the useless items aside, Tom moved cautiously forward. Suddenly he stepped on something that rolled underneath his foot. He crashed to the ground with a yell of alarm.

'Are you all right?' asked Sarah.

'I think so,' said Tom grumpily.

He found that he was lying on something – the object that had tripped him.

Picking it up, he got to his feet and examined it. 'I don't believe it!' he whispered. 'If only it works.'

Suddenly a powerful beam of light sprang out from the object. Tom swung it round on the astonished Sarah.

He was holding a torch – one of those massive, industrial-sized ones with a rubber cover. It felt wet and sticky to the touch for some reason – but it worked!

'Talk about luck,' he said. 'Now we're in business!'

'But what was it doing lying there on the floor?' asked Sarah.

Tom thought for a moment. 'I think it belonged to someone who was doing what we're doing – looking round. Looking round for what he could find. For some reason he lost his torch and couldn't find it again.'

'Yes, but how did he come to lose it?'

'I've got a theory about that as well,' said Tom grimly. Taking the torch in one hand he shone the beam on his other hand. The hand was covered with a reddish-brown smear.

The stickiness on the torch was blood.

CHAPTER FOUR

KILLER

TOM SWUNG the torch beam round until he found a pile of towels. He used one of them to clean his hand and the torch as best he could.

'Looks as if there was a pretty nasty struggle,' he said. 'Whoever used to own this torch must have been the one who lost!'

Sarah looked around, wondering what dangers lurked in the cavernous darkness.

'Let's get what we need and get out of here,' she said.

'Right,' said Tom. 'What we need right now is a store guide.'

They found a store guide and Tom played the torch over it.

'Outdoor sports clothing is the kind of stuff we need,' he said. 'The sort of things people wear for skiing and mountain-climbing and all that outdoor survival sort of activity. You know all about that stuff, Sarah, you can pick something out for us.'

It was a subject Sarah was very knowledgeable about. 'I wonder if they'll have those special fabrics they had in our world?' she said. 'Light and strong and waterproof. Clothes that keep you warm or cold according to the outside temperature.'

Tom shrugged. 'Who knows?' That was the trouble with alternative universes. Some things were drastically different, others exactly the same. 'I expect there's something like that here,' he said. 'Wear your anorak with pride!'

They climbed the motionless escalators to the sports department on the second floor. It was pretty clear that others had been there before them. Shelves and display cases had been emptied and clothes lay scattered over the floor. But after some searching they found the kind of clothes they were looking for, still in their boxes in a little storeroom.

Thankfully they changed their wet clothes for trousers and hooded anoraks, made from one of the miracle materials that Sarah had described. They put on dry socks and sweaters and comfortable walking boots as well.

They found a couple of lightweight rucksacks, and packed some spare clothes inside.

Remembering the blood on the torch, Tom looked around for some kind of weapon. The display cases that might once have held knives etc. were all smashed and empty.

If civilisation really has broken down, thought Tom, weapons would be the first things to go.

All he managed to find was what looked like the latest thing in Swiss Army knives, with gadgets for every possible emergency and a compass built into the handle.

He stuck it in his pocket and turned to Sarah. 'Got everything you want?'

Sarah looked down at her mountaineering outfit and smiled wryly. It was, she thought, a lot more practical than it was glamorous. 'I wouldn't mind picking up a little black dress for evening wear, but I don't suppose there's much point.'

'Food next, then,' said Tom. 'And drink, of course. Maybe some bottles and tins and packets of dried stuff have survived.'

'Food hall's back down on the ground floor,' said Sarah.

They descended to the first floor and rooted about among the wrecked shelves and cabinets. They had been almost completely looted, but Sarah and Tom managed to find some tins of meat and a few cans of fruit.

Tom opened a can of peaches with the tin-opener on his Swiss Army knife. They sat down on the floor and ate them from the can with their fingers.

After a moment, Sarah said, 'Aren't there any *nice* alternative worlds anywhere? Ones where things went even better than in our one?'

'I suppose there must be,' said Tom. 'According to your theory, everything that can happen does happen in some alternative dimension. So that means . . .'

Suddenly a voice bellowed from the surrounding darkness. 'Looting, eh? Don't move!'

Tom grabbed the torch and they both jumped up. He swept the torch-beam round towards the voice and illuminated a terrifying figure.

Standing not far away was a huge, gaunt, bearded man in a ragged coat. He had a bow in his hand, with an arrow drawn back and ready to fire.

Whoever he is, he doesn't look much like the police, thought Tom.

'We only took what we needed,' he said out loud. 'It looks as if lots of others have done the same thing.'

'This is my store now!' roared the giant. 'Anything you take, you pay me! I've already shot one of you looter rats today, and now here are two more!'

'Who says it's your store?' asked Sarah.

'This does!'

An arrow flashed between them and stuck quivering in the oak-panelled wall of the food hall. Before they could even react, the giant had another arrow in the bow, and was ready to fire again.

'Well?' he growled.

'Well what?' said Tom.

'What's it to be? Pay for that stuff or put it back!'

'I don't suppose you take Credcards?' asked Tom.

'Gold or goods,' snarled the man. 'Pay up!'

'We can't,' said Sarah. 'We've got nothing to pay you with.'

'Then put it all back!'

'We can't do that either,' said Tom. 'We need everything we've taken to survive.'

'Why don't you just let us go?' asked Sarah. 'We only took these clothes and a little food. We won't come back again.'

'Can't do that,' said the giant. 'I'll have to make an example of you. Stand still and I'll make it quick and clean. Don't go dodging about like that other one. He crawled away to die like a wounded rat!'

'Rat yourself!' screamed a high, scratchy voice.

Something metallic and shiny flashed from the darkness and struck the giant on the head with a solid clunk.

He groaned and slumped to the ground, dropping the bow.

A ragged little figure appeared and grabbed Tom's arm. 'Quick, hold him down, I'll strangle him before he wakes up!'

Sarah was horrified. 'You can't do that!'

'Why not?' The man pointed to a dark, wet patch on the sleeve of his coat. 'He tried to kill me. He'd have killed you if I hadn't clobbered him with that can of tomatoes. Waste of good food!' Something caught his attention. 'Here, that's my torch!'

'Take it!' said Tom. He thrust the torch into the man's hand. 'Let's get out of here before he comes round.'

The giant was already struggling to get up. There was

blood on his forehead and he looked in a very bad mood.

'Too late now anyway,' said the ragged man. 'All right, come on.' He switched off the torch, plunging them into gloom.

Tom grabbed the tail of his overcoat with one hand and Sarah's hand with the other. They hurried off into the blackness.

Led by their strange new guide, they moved along the darkened aisles of the big store. He seemed to know his way perfectly well despite the darkness, and led them across the store, down a flight of stone steps, along a dark corridor and finally into some kind of room.

He went over to a corner, there was the flare of a match, and then a yellow glow from an oil lamp. He put the lamp on a rickety table and they looked around.

They were in a smallish stone-walled room – it looked as if it had once been a basement storeroom. It was furnished with an amazingly varied assortment of odds and ends. There was a mattress on the floor, an armchair, a table and a scattering of chairs. There was a wooden table piled high with cans of food. There were mirrors, pictures and all kind of ornaments on shelves around the room.

He's like a magpie, thought Sarah. Picking up and hiding away anything that takes his fancy!

'Like a cuppa?' said the man unexpectedly. 'Take a seat.' He lit a spirit stove under a kettle and produced a packet of tea, a tin of milk and a few cups and mugs.

Tom and Sarah sat down on rickety wooden chairs and

studied their new host.

He was a ratty-looking little man in a long, ragged overcoat and ancient wellington boots. He seemed to be wearing several layers of garments under the overcoat. A long, sharp nose and a straggly beard added to the rat-like appearance.

He looked up and saw that they were watching him. 'Name's Jimmy,' he said, giving them a largely toothless grin.

'Tom,' said Tom. 'This is my cousin Sarah. Thanks for helping us. Nice little place you've got here.'

'Not bad, is it?' said Jimmy proudly.

'Is it . . . safe?' asked Tom.

'What? Oh, Big Sid, you mean? No, he doesn't know about my little nest. He never comes down here.'

'I take it Big Sid was that character with the bow and arrows upstairs,' said Sarah. 'Who does he think he is, saying this is his store?'

'Well, all the big stores have blokes like that hanging around,' said Jimmy. 'Sometimes it's gangs, and that's worse. Big Sid's too bad-tempered to have a gang. He had one once but he killed half of them off and the rest ran away.' He rubbed his bristly chin. 'Mind you, I reckon we were right not to kill him.'

'Of course we were,' said Sarah. 'You can't go around doing that sort of thing.'

'Oh yes I could,' said Jimmy. 'But would I be any better off?'

'Better the devil you know, you mean?' said Tom.

'That's right. Big Sid's a nasty piece of work but there's only one of him – and he's stupid, easy to fool. And he keeps the others away. If I knocked him off someone else would only move in. Maybe someone worse.'

Tom and Sarah looked at each other, sharing the same thought. It was hard to imagine someone worse than Big Sid.

'Suppose he does come down here?' asked Sarah.

'Well, we've hurt his pride now, haven't we?' said Jimmy. 'If he finds us now, he'll kill us. He'll kill us all.'

CHAPTER FIVE

AMBUSH

DESPITE HIS gruesome prophecy, Jimmy seemed quite unworried. Tom and Sarah watched him as he went on happily with his tea-making.

The kettle was boiling by now, and Jimmy made tea in a big brown pot with a broken spout. He poured it out and added milk from a tin with two holes in the top.

He passed cups of tea to Tom and Sarah. 'Sugar in that tin there if you want it. Help yourself.'

'How long have things been like this?' asked Sarah, as she sipped her tea.

Jimmy looked puzzled. 'Like what?'

'London flooded, everyone moved out . . .'

Jimmy scratched his shaggy head. 'Seems like for ever. I suppose things were different when I was younger but that was years ago. Seems like another world.'

'What happened exactly?' asked Tom. 'How did it all start?'

Jimmy stared suspiciously at him. 'Don't you know?'

'We've come from a long way away,' said Sarah. 'From abroad. We didn't expect to find anything like this.'

'Can you remember what happened when things first started to go wrong?' asked Tom gently.

Jimmy scratched his head again, harder this time. 'How did it all start?' he said. 'Hard to say. I was only a nipper then, anyway.'

'Try to remember,' pleaded Sarah. 'We'd really like to know what happened. It's very important to us.'

'How did it all start?' Jimmy swigged noisily at his tea. 'One minute everything was fine. It was all peace and prosperity for years and years. We had all this high-tech stuff. It was so cheap that everybody could afford it. Everyone had pocket computers and mobile phones and all kinds of gadgets, even the kids. Even the poorest people had cars and the rich families had two or three. There was plenty of cheap food, business was booming, everybody seemed rich and happy.'

'Was anyone worried about the way things were going?' asked Sarah. 'The environment, that sort of thing?'

Jimmy shrugged. 'Oh, a few people were banging on about pollution and global warming and scientists mucking about with our food but nobody took much notice. Then it all started to crack up. The weather went funny first. Warm winters and cold summers, all sorts of things. Then the floods came. Down here in the south copped it worse, it wasn't so bad up north. And there was all these new

40

diseases nobody could cure. For some reason the medicines didn't seem to work any more. They called these new illnesses the new plagues. There was two or three of them, each one worse than the last. Millions of people died – all my own family went. I had a bad go myself, but I got over it. I seemed to be all right after that, none of the other plagues touched me.'

'Didn't any other countries help?' asked Tom. 'Send supplies and aid and all that sort of thing?'

'They did for a while,' said Jimmy. 'Lot of stuff come over from America on relief planes. Then they couldn't help much any more because it started happening to them as well. The weather was going wrong all over the world. Farming was going wrong everywhere too, all the plants and animals turned funny. We saw it all on the telly – when there was still any telly. It packed up after a while. We had the radio for a bit and then that went too . . .'

'What happened then?' asked Sarah.

'Pretty well everything,' said Jimmy simply. 'There was more plagues, lots more people dying. The floods and the diseases got worse and those who survived left London.'

'Where did they go?' asked Tom.

'Somewhere up north, I suppose,' said Jimmy vaguely. 'Most of the south-east and the west country is under water. There's supposed to be some kind of government up north but they don't interfere down here. They let us alone, and we let them alone.'

'Did you ever hear of something called transmat?' asked Sarah.

Jimmy shook his head. 'Not so far as I know.'

'Back when you were younger maybe?' suggested Tom.

'Hang on a minute . . . transmat. Wasn't that the new gimmick they demonstrated at the Millennium Science Pavilion? Supposed to send people whizzing through space like a radio message?'

'That's right,' said Sarah eagerly. 'Did you see the demonstration?'

'No, but I saw it on telly. Quite early on, that was. Talk about a performance!'

Tom and Sarah looked anxiously at each other. 'What happened?' asked Tom.

Jimmy laughed. 'They sent off all these different objects at first. A coffee pot, some books. Supposed to transfer them from one glass dome to another ten metres away. Some things never arrived at all, and those that did were smashed up. The coffee pot was busted and all the books ripped to shreds. But that wasn't the worst of it. Guess what happened next?'

'Tell us,' said Sarah.

'They sent off this poor little rabbit and this duck – both together, it was!'

'What happened to them?' asked Tom. 'Were they killed?'

'Worse than that! They arrived all mixed up. Two weird creatures, part rabbit and part duck! Only lived a few minutes, poor things.'

'I don't suppose anyone fancied a trip by transmat very much after that,' said Tom.

'What happened to the scientists working on it?' asked Sarah.

'Everyone just laughed at them. They swore they could get it right in time, but nobody believed them. Then all the other troubles started coming along and everyone forgot about it.'

'Nobody tried to get it going again, later on?' asked Tom.

'Wouldn't have been safe, would it? Not later on . . .'

'Why not?'

'Cause of the riots.'

'What riots?' asked Sarah.

'The anti-science riots. People started blaming scientists for everything that had gone wrong. Scientists were being locked up, beaten up, hunted down and killed outright before the end.'

Jimmy gave a hacking cough. 'All this talking's making me dry. I'll put some more hot water on the tea.'

He went over to the other side of the room and busied himself with the tea things. Tom and Sarah looked at each other.

'Scapegoats,' whispered Sarah. 'They turned the scientists into scapegoats.'

'People always need someone to blame,' said Tom quietly. 'Apart from themselves, that is! Though I suppose science was at least partly responsible.'

'Irresponsible, reckless science maybe,' said Sarah. 'But what about the people who encouraged it, profited from it? And to turn against every kind of science – it's just mad.'

'Anyway, I was right,' said Tom. 'For what it's worth. Transmat *was* invented.'

Sarah nodded. 'Let's hope they carried on working on it in secret somewhere and eventually got it right.'

'Well,' said Tom. 'If we don't manage to find our family, I suppose we'll just have to take a trip up north and see what we can find out!'

Jimmy turned round just in time to catch the last few words. 'Go north?' he said, horrified. 'You don't wanna do that.'

'Things might be a bit better up there.'

'Ah yes, but what about getting there? You'd have to go through the middle bit. It's a wasteland out there. There's bandits and monsters and all sorts. Why not stay here where you're safe?'

'You call this safe?' said Sarah. 'Dodging round this ruined store with that loony upstairs trying to kill you!'

'Look, I've got it cushy compared to most,' said Jimmy indignantly. 'Place to sleep, plenty of food . . . See, there's hardly anyone left in London now, so even though there's not much left, there's still enough to go round.'

'There's a government of sorts in the north,' said Tom. 'You said so yourself. Some kind of civilisation.'

'If you can reach it alive. And who knows what it'll be like when you find it? Tell you what, you can stay here

44

with me. We'll form our own gang. And if Big Sid gets to be too much of a nuisance we'll knock him off while he's asleep.'

Jimmy looked at them eagerly. There was something pathetic about his eagerness for their company. He must have been alone a long time. 'Come on, what do you say?'

Tom and Sarah exchanged looks. As usual, each knew what the other was thinking.

'I'm sorry,' said Sarah gently. 'Thanks for the tea and all the help but we've got to be moving along. There's a chance our family may still be living in our old house – we've got to go and find out first, before we do anything else. But I want to take a look at that arm of yours before we go.'

'Arm's all right,' muttered Jimmy. 'Just a scratch, I've had much worse than that.'

'I'm taking a look all the same,' said Sarah. 'Have you got any first-aid stuff?'

'Box over there in the corner.'

Tom went and got the box while Sarah made Jimmy take off his overcoat, and the coat underneath and pushed back the sleeve of his tattered shirt. The arrow had cut a shallow gash across the top his scrawny arm, just below the left shoulder.

'Doesn't look too bad,' said Sarah. 'That overcoat must have protected you like a suit of armour. I'd better clean it up for you, though.'

Ignoring Jimmy's yells of protest, she swabbed the wound clean with water from the kettle, dusted on some antiseptic powder, and put on a dressing and a bandage, covering the lot with sticking plaster.

Jimmy plunged thankfully back into his long overcoat like a tortoise getting back into its shell. It occurred to Tom that he probably hadn't taken it off for years.

Sarah rinsed her hands with the remainder of the hot water. 'Well, we'd better get moving,' she said.

'I still think you're mad,' said Jimmy. 'Still, if you must. Here, take this . . .'

He began sorting out cans and packets from his food supply. 'You want to concentrate on stuff like tinned fruit and tomatoes,' he explained. 'Gives you food and drink all in one go.'

'We can't take your supplies,' protested Tom. 'You must be running out by now.'

Jimmy sniffed. 'There's still enough left if you know where to look. And if I can't find what I want here, I'll take my custom to Harrods!'

When their packs were loaded he said gruffly, 'Come on, then, I'll show you a safe way out. You don't want to risk another run-in with Big Sid!'

He led them out of the little room, along more corridors, and finally to a door that opened on to a long, cobbled alleyway full of dustbins and wooden hatchways.

'This is right round the back,' he explained. 'Delivery area. Go straight down the alleyway, turn right and then left and you'll be heading north!' He held out a grimy hand. 'Well, goodbye. And the best of luck!'

'Goodbye,' said Tom, shaking hands.

'Goodbye,' said Sarah. 'And thanks again.' She shook Jimmy's hand and planted a quick kiss on his whiskery cheek.

'Very touching,' growled a hateful voice. 'Well, now it's goodbye for all of you!'

Big Sid was standing in a doorway on the other side of the alleyway, covering them with an arrow in his already-drawn bow.

Beside him, on top of a crate, was a bundle of arrows.

He looked, Sarah realised, like someone set up for target practice.

And they were the targets . . .

CHAPTER SIX

DEATH RUN

'DIDN'T KNOW I'd found your other rat-hole, did you, Jimmy?' sneered Big Sid triumphantly. 'Well, I've been keeping track of your comings and goings, you little rat. I thought you might bring your new friends out this way. And you fell for it!'

Nobody spoke.

Tom and Sarah couldn't think of anything useful to say.

Jimmy just stood there, frozen in terror.

Tom and Sarah looked around, trying to find some chance of escape.

He can only shoot one arrow at a time, Tom was thinking. However quick he is, there's a chance for us between shots. Not much of a chance, though . . .

Tom remembered how quickly Big Sid had fitted another arrow to the bow after firing his warning shot between them in the store. He looked quickly at Sarah. He knew that she was thinking much the same thing. He gave the tiniest of nods, and she nodded back.

To move too soon would be fatal.

Big Sid would use the bow and arrow to kill the first one to jump him – and probably the second as well. Then he'd use the machete stuck in his belt to kill the third.

Even if they did dodge his arrows, he was too big to take on. Killing all three of them separately or together would give him no trouble at all.

The only thing to do was wait – wait for the slightest opportunity, and seize it when it came.

Big Sid seemed disappointed by the lack of response to his dramatic arrival. 'Well?' he snarled. 'Got nothing to say for yourselves?'

He wants to spin it out a bit, thought Tom. He's having such a good time he doesn't want it to end too quickly!

'You seem to enjoy doing all the talking,' said Tom. 'I'd hate to spoil your fun.'

'I'll have my fun all right,' snarled Big Sid. 'Don't you worry about that. Now, move out here away from that doorway, the lot of you. Don't want you ducking back inside, do we? Come right out into the middle of the alley.'

There seemed no choice but to obey.

Big Sid stared menacingly at them.

With an effort, Tom managed a fairly convincing yawn. 'Well? What next?'

If I can make him angry, thought Tom, he might just get careless.

It didn't work.

'I'll tell you what's next,' said Big Sid, quite calmly. 'I'm going to give you all a sporting chance.'

'That's very kind of you,' said Sarah. 'What sort of a chance?'

'There's a little game that was invented especially for the benefit of looters. It's called the Death Run.'

Tom made an effort to keep his voice calm. 'Really? I like a good game. What are the rules?'

There was gloating cruelty in the giant's voice. 'Oh, the rules are simple enough – dead simple, you might say. You three run for the other end of the alleyway – one by one. Anybody who makes it out of the alleyway alive gets to go on living.'

Sarah looked at him unbelievingly. 'You're not serious, are you? What sort of a chance is that? You can't just kill us in cold blood!'

'We could have killed you earlier on, when Jimmy knocked you out,' said Tom. 'But we didn't, we let you live.'

'More fool you,' said Big Sid brutally. 'Now, who's going to go first?'

'Me!' said Sarah. She was pretty sure she was the fastest-moving and most nimble of the three. If she could dodge Sid's arrows, it would give Tom and Jimmy a chance to run.

Before she could move, Jimmy yelled, 'No, me! Run for it, you two!'

He began stumbling down the alleyway in a jerky run, his long ragged overcoat flapping around him.

Tom and Sarah watched in horror as Big Sid tracked the movement of the running figure with his arrowhead.

It was clear that Jimmy was going to make a very easy target.

They saw Big Sid draw back the arrow the last few centimetres, the bowstring taut, ready to fire.

Tom looked around desperately for a weapon. He grabbed the lid of a nearby dustbin and spun it across the alleyway like a giant Frisbee. It hit Big Sid across the chest, spoiling his aim and knocking the bow from his hands.

'Quick, Sarah, run!' yelled Tom.

Big Sid gave a roar of rage and pulled the machete from his belt.

Tom and Sarah dashed down the alleyway after Jimmy, Big Sid pounding behind them. For a man his size he moved amazingly fast.

As they ran, Tom and Sarah grabbed dustbins and old boxes, throwing them in front of their pursuer in a desperate attempt to slow him down.

He dodged the missiles with apparent ease.

He was getting closer . . .

Near the mouth of the alleyway, Tom turned and rolled the last dustbin at Big Sid's legs.

Big Sid leaped high in the air. He soared effortlessly over the rolling obstacle, and thudded down on the wooden hatchway on its other side.

The old wooden hatchway shattered beneath his weight and he disappeared.

There was a terrible scream, a thud, and then silence.

Tom stopped, gasping, and went to the edge of the shattered hatchway. Sarah stopped running too and came back to join him.

Cautiously they peered over the edge. They were looking down a deep stone shaft, with a motionless figure at the bottom.

Jimmy came staggering up and looked as well.

'Well, that's the end of him,' he said with satisfaction. 'That's the delivery chute, goes straight down to the deepest cellar. They used to lower beer and wine barrels down there.'

'The hatchway must have rotted over the years,' said Tom. 'Besides, he came down on it with a terrific thump.'

'Good riddance,' said Jimmy. 'Well, you paid me back for helping you all right. He'd have skewered me with his little bow and arrow that time. I'd have been as dead as Cock Robin!'

'Who?' asked Tom.

'It's an old nursery rhyme,' said Sarah. She recited it:

'Who killed Cock Robin?
"I," said the sparrow,
"With my bow and arrow
I killed Cock Robin!"

'And talking of bows and arrows . . .'

She went back up the alleyway and picked up the bow

and examined it. 'It's a modern hunting bow, fibreglass and nylon.' She looked at Jimmy. 'I think I'll have this if you don't mind.'

He shuddered. 'You're welcome to it.'

'He left some more arrows up there,' said Tom.

Sarah slung the bow over one shoulder.

Tom looked curiously at her. 'I thought you didn't approve of weapons?'

'I still don't,' said Sarah. 'But I don't approve of getting killed by some thug like Big Sid either.'

Tom went and collected the bundle of arrows from the top of the crate and tucked them under the flap of Sarah's rucksack.

'Well, goodbye again,' he said. 'Good luck, Jimmy!'

Jimmy gave him an anguished look. 'You don't have to go right away, do you? It's late afternoon already. How far can you get before it gets dark? If you don't reach your home in time you'll have to find somewhere safe and dry to sleep, wake up cold and hungry . . .'

It was clear that the old man was desperate for company. But Tom realised that there was a lot of sense in what Jimmy said. Somehow setting off into the unknown under that dark and cloudy sky didn't seem very appealing.

'Stay the night here,' Jimmy went on. 'I can give you a good meal and a warm bed and you can set off bright and early in the morning.'

Tom looked at Sarah. 'What do you think?'

'It makes sense to me.' She looked at the gaping

hatchway and shuddered. 'I think I've had enough excitement for one day.'

Jimmy got out the best of his provisions and they had a splendid supper of tinned chicken, tinned vegetables and tinned fruit, washed down with genuine tinned Coke.

'This store's been the saving of me,' he said. 'I had a job here, see, just before things got really bad. Delivery boy, porter, general dogsbody. I got to know the place inside out. So when things finally collapsed I just sort of moved in.'

'Didn't anyone else get the same idea?' asked Tom.

'Place got looted, of course, just like everywhere else. But by that time there weren't many people left. Most just took what they could carry and cleared off. I kept out of the way till they'd gone.'

'I'm surprised the store hasn't been completely cleared out by now,' said Sarah.

'Well a heck of a lot of stuff has gone, but the place is so huge there's still enough left to keep me going. Of course, there was always Big Sid to worry about – up till now, anyway!'

'What about other thugs like Sid?' asked Tom.

'There's still quite a few left – I'll have to take my chances,' admitted Jimmy. 'But they're more on the outskirts of London than in the centre. They roam round picking up what they can find – robbing anyone they can find, come to that. And they fight each other as well, over loot and territory. One day they'll wipe each other out and leave me in peace.' He paused. 'Thought any more about what I said earlier? About staying on here with me permanent? You can see, it's not a bad life!'

Once again, Tom and Sarah shared the same thought. To both of them it seemed like a terrible life. Living like a rat in a ruined store, dodging bandits and bullies . . .

But they didn't want to hurt Jimmy's feelings.

'It's very kind of you, Jimmy,' said Sarah gently. 'But tomorrow morning we really must be off. We've got to try to find our family if we can. We've got places to go and things to do.'

The chances of finding their family were pretty remote, thought Tom. And those places and things were pretty vague. But Sarah was right. They had to try to find some answer to all their problems. Staying here would simply be giving up.

However great the dangers ahead, they had to go on.

Somehow they just had to find a way to get back to their own world, their own home . . .

JOURNEY TO DANGER

THEY SLEPT the night in the store's bedding department, with dozens of beds to choose from. Early next morning, after a breakfast of tinned bacon and pickled eggs they said their farewells.

'Well, goodbye again,' said Jimmy. 'And good luck! Remember, you can always come back again, if things don't work out.'

'Thanks,' said Sarah. 'We'll remember that.'

As they moved off along Oxford Street, they turned for a last look back.

Jimmy stood outside the store – his store – waving frantically for a moment, and then disappeared inside.

They went on their way.

As they walked along the muddy, rubble-strewn Oxford Street, Sarah said, 'The weather's improved a bit.'

The sky was still dark and overcast, and the air thick, but there was no sign of the acrid fog that had hung over the flooded Trafalgar Square. The rain had stopped, and so had the thunder and lightning.

'It's only improved from ghastly to terrible,' said Tom. 'Do you think it's always like this?'

'No idea. If these climate changes *are* caused by global warming things could be, well, changeable. We might be in for anything from bright sunshine to snowstorms, all in the space of a few hours!'

'Just the usual English weather, then?'

'That's right,' agreed Sarah. 'Only more and worse!'

They turned left at the battered ruin of the Dominion Theatre and headed due north.

As they got further from the centre the signs of devastation grew worse. Big buildings like department stores and office blocks had survived pretty well, but many of the smaller ones had collapsed completely.

It was a depressing scene, and it lowered Tom's spirits. 'I'm beginning to wonder exactly what we're doing,' he said.

Sarah gave him a surprised look. 'I thought we'd agreed to go home and look for our family?'

'And if we don't find them?'

'We keep on going north.'

'Yes, but why?'

'Because south, east and west are mostly under water – according to Jimmy, anyway. There doesn't seem to be anything left in London but deserted buildings, ruins and robbers, so we don't want to stay there. That only leaves north.'

'So what are we looking for?'

'Anything we can find,' said Sarah. 'Jimmy says there's supposed to be some kind of government up there, remember. Where there's civilisation there might be scientists.'

'We're placing a lot of reliance on Jimmy,' grumbled Tom.

'We've got to. He's the only person we've met who hasn't tried to kill us! If we meet some more people maybe we can get some better information.'

Suddenly three people appeared on the road ahead. They came out of a ruined pub and they were clutching bottles.

'These three don't look too promising,' said Tom.

Sarah slipped the bow from her shoulder. Reaching over her shoulder she took an arrow from her pack.

The men had noticed them by now and were staggering towards them in a loose semi-circle. As they came closer Tom and Sarah saw that all three looked much alike. All three were thin, gaunt and rickety, like the survivors of some terrible disease. They were dirty, ragged and savage-looking and each of them had a weapon of some kind in one hand and a bottle in the other.

One carried a home-made spear, the second had a machete, and the third had a wooden club.

They looked weak and half-starved, but extremely dangerous.

They came to a halt and the one in the middle, who

seemed to be the leader, held up his hand – the one with the machete.

'Halt!' he said in a thick, slurred voice. 'If you want to go any further you got to pay the toll.'

Tom studied the scruffy little group. Even though they were armed, they were all half-drunk. But then there were three of them. Maybe he could get rid of them at the cost of a tin of fruit.

'How much is the toll?' he asked.

The one with the spear giggled. 'Everything you've got!'

'Too much,' said Sarah.

She had an arrow fitted to the bow by now, the bowstring drawn back, the arrow ready to fire.

The leader took a step forwards, machete raised threateningly.

'That's far enough,' snapped Sarah. 'Take another step and I'll kill you – and the other two before they can reach us.'

Tom shoved his hand deep into his pocket, doing his best to make his still-folded Swiss Army knife look like a gun.

'And if she doesn't get the last one, I will!' he snarled.

The three men hesitated.

Then the one with the club growled, 'He's not got any gun there, he's bluffing. They're only a couple of kids. Let's get 'em!'

Raising his club he sprang forward.

Instantly Sarah fired.

The arrow struck the wooden club in the man's hand so hard that it knocked it from his grasp.

At the same moment Tom bounded forwards, wrenched the machete from the leader's hand and raised it threateningly.

That left just the third man, the one with the spear.

He made a half-hearted attempt to raise the weapon – only to find that Sarah already had another arrow in her bow and was covering him.

'Drop it!' she snapped.

He dropped it.

For a moment everyone stood there like waxworks.

Then the leader snarled, 'All right, you win. Don't spin it out, get on with it. Just make it quick, it's good and sharp.'

He glared defiantly at Tom over the blade of the machete.

With sudden horror Tom realised that the man was expecting to be killed.

Tom stepped back beside Sarah, keeping the machete raised. 'We're not going to kill you,' he said. 'Not this time. Just clear off while you can.'

'No!' said Sarah.

The leader swung round on her. 'You're the bloodthirsty one, are you?' he sneered. 'They say the women are the worst. What is it, the Death Run? Well, you can forget it, I'm not trying to outrun no arrow. If you're going to skewer me, you do it right here, at close range. Only like I told your boyfriend, just make it quick!'

'Don't tempt me,' said Sarah. 'Don't worry, I don't want to kill you. Just answer some questions!'

'Why should I?'

'Because I'll kill you if you don't!' screamed Sarah. She took a step towards him, drawing back the bowstring. 'Start talking!'

The leader stepped back, raising his hands. 'All right, all right!' he growled. 'What questions?'

'What are things like up ahead? Are we likely to meet any more specimens like you?'

'Not for quite a way. This is our territory, such as it is. Get past us and nobody much will bother you.'

'And further on?' asked Tom.

'I doubt it. Pickings are pretty poor round this way, not many gangs bother. How far are you going?'

'Hampstead, first,' said Sarah. 'After that, as far as we can get. Right up north if we can make it.'

'No chance,' said the man decisively. 'You'll have to get past the heath if you're heading north. You'll never make it.'

'Hampstead Heath?' asked Tom. 'I've walked over it plenty of times.'

'Have you? When?'

'Well, not for quite a while.'

'You may find it's changed a bit, sonny. Anything else?'

'Have you heard anything about any kind of

government – further north?'

'You hear all sorts of tales. Soldiers, monsters, black magicians. I reckon it's safer back here. Is that it?'

Tom looked at Sarah.

She nodded. 'That'll do. Clear off! Don't get any ideas because we let you off this time. Bother us again and we'll kill the lot of you.'

'Yeah, sure,' said the leader. He turned to Tom. 'Any chance I can get the machete back? I've done a lot of work on it.'

Tom looked down at the weapon in his hand. It had a leather-bound hilt, a brass guard and a long, curved blade that looked razor sharp. He shook his head. 'Sorry, spoils of war. Besides, my need is greater than yours.'

'It is if you're going across the heath,' said the gang leader with a jeering laugh. He turned to his two bemused henchmen. 'Come on, you useless lot. You're no good with kids. Let's see if we can find some old lady to scare!'

Still clutching their bottles, the three men staggered off.

Tom and Sarah stood watching them until they were too far away to be any danger.

Tom turned to Sarah. 'Well done – you were very convincing. You even scared me!'

'I scared myself!' said Sarah.

'I thought you were just bluffing – but you really can shoot that thing. How come?'

'At the academy for young ladies I once attended, there

was a sort of retro craze for the noble art of toxophily.'

'Come again?'

'We did archery. I was school champion.'

Sarah's voice was a little shaky and Tom gave her a look of concern. 'You all right?'

'Just about. That was pretty nasty for a while.' She paused. 'Thank goodness they gave up. I don't know if I could actually shoot someone.'

'Maybe it won't come to that,' said Tom consolingly. He grinned. 'Let's just concentrate on looking so tough that nobody dares bother us.'

They went on their way, moving towards the unknown dangers that lay ahead.

THE DEADLY HEATH

'I WONDER what that man meant about the heath?' said Tom. 'He seemed to be saying it was dangerous now.'

It was some time later and they'd been trudging through the desolate cityscape for several hours. As the road climbed the signs of flood damage faded away. They were moving towards one of the highest parts of London now, and it didn't look as if the flood waters had reached this far. But the houses seemed empty and deserted, and there was an eerie silence all around them.

'Perhaps it's got overgrown,' said Sarah.

'It always was!'

That was the whole point about the heath. It was far more like a stretch of open country than a formal park. Tom and Sarah had lived quite close to it in their own universe. They'd spent a lot of time playing on it when they were younger.

'I suppose there might be dangerous animals – wild

dogs or something like that,' suggested Sarah. 'Anyway, we'll find out soon. We're pretty close to home.'

Tom nodded. 'That's East Heath Road just over there.'

East Heath Road ran right along the edge of the heath. They crossed a deserted little square and the railway bridge on the other side but then stopped in amazement.

The edge of the heath was in sight by now – but it wasn't the heath they knew. Instead of rolling open countryside and the familiar line of little ponds, all they could see was a sort of dense green thicket.

'It's overgrown all right,' said Tom. 'But overgrown with what? Trees?'

'Too small for trees,' said Sarah. 'But too big for plants – any normal plants, anyway. Let's take a closer look.'

They walked to the edge of the thicket. Seen from close to it consisted of densely-packed plants, huge plants with thick stems and massive leaves.'

'What are they?' asked Sarah.

Tom shook his head. 'Nothing I've ever seen before.'

He tried to thrust his way between them. It was possible to force your way through, but only just. He stepped back.

'It's like dense jungle. You could get through it if you had to, I suppose, carve your way through with a machete. But it's like the Amazon rainforest in there. You'd be lost in no time.'

'Listen,' said Sarah.

Tom listened. 'I can't hear anything.'

'That's what I mean. I don't think I've seen or even heard any kind of bird or animal since we arrived.'

'Maybe they've all died out . . .'

Suddenly there was a rustling and stirring in the thick green growth. Tom stepped back cautiously – and a nightmarish creature rushed out at him. He got a quick confused impression of fierce red eyes and savage jaws.

It was a rat.

A rat as big as a dog.

Tom jumped back with a yell of alarm, snatched the machete from his belt and lashed down at it.

He lopped its head clean off at a stroke.

Horribly, the jaws on the severed head went on snapping, and the claws scrabbled frantically on the headless body. The thing didn't seem to know it was dead.

Another giant rat sprang out of the thick undergrowth, leaping for Tom's throat. It fell, squealing, transfixed by Sarah's arrow.

More giant rats appeared from the dense green thicket. They flung themselves not on Tom but on their dead fellow creatures, tearing them to pieces.

More rats appeared and then more, and these headed for Tom and Sarah. They turned to run back down the hill, but the rats had surged across the road in a straggling line, barring their retreat.

They were forced to run *up* the steep hill instead – with the angry rats snapping at their heels.

It flashed through Tom's mind that this was a deliberate

tactic. The rats chased their prey uphill to tire it quicker.

Which showed a worrying degree of intelligence . . .

'Keep running, Sarah!' yelled Tom. 'Look for shelter. I'll try to hold them back!'

As he ran, Tom stopped and turned from time to time, slashing wildly down at the approaching horde. Each rat he killed or wounded bought them a little more time as the rest of the rats stopped to devour it.

But each respite was brief, and soon the rats were on the trail again – and Tom and Sarah were getting tired.

'If we could get into a building and bar the door,' gasped Sarah.

But there were no buildings in reach.

'Sarah, listen, there's an old block of flats halfway up the hill!' shouted Tom. He stopped and slashed savagely at the rats again and then went on running.

In his heart he knew they'd never make it in time.

Suddenly an extraordinary shape came whizzing down the hill towards them. For a moment Tom thought it was some kind of mechanical monster – but it turned out to be a man in a black leather outfit on a huge motorbike and sidecar combination. He had some kind of tank in the combination and a nozzle in his hands. He stopped the bike level with Tom and Sarah and began spraying something from the nozzle over the rats.

They curled up and collapsed, writhing, and the survivors flung themselves on their bodies.

'Quick, get on!' yelled the man. 'Get on top of the sidecar!'

Somehow Tom and Sarah scrambled on board. They clung on precariously as the motorcyclist gave the rats a final blast from his spray, wheeled the bike and sidecar in a circle and zoomed back up the hill.

He drove up to the block of flats Tom had mentioned, through the open gates and into a garage at the side of the block.

'We'd better get upstairs,' he said, climbing off the bike. He looked a sinister figure in black leathers and goggles, but the voice was unexpectedly high and squeaky. 'They hate to give up a scent.'

Tom and Sarah followed him up several fights of steps into a comfortably furnished top-floor flat with a good view over the overgrown heath. A telescope on a tripod stood before the big picture window.

He took off his goggles and leathers, revealing a tubby, white-bearded, benign-looking man in sports jacket and flannels.

Taking off their packs, Tom and Sarah collapsed, gasping, into armchairs.

'Thanks!' said Sarah. 'You saved our lives. What were those horrible things?'

'Mutated rats,' said their rescuer. 'They're all over the place these days. They nest in the hogweed and dash out to attack anything edible that passes by. Didn't anyone tell you the heath was dangerous?'

'Somebody did try to warn us as a matter of fact,' said Tom. 'We should have paid more attention.'

'I saw you being attacked through my telescope,' the man went on. 'You didn't look too much like bandits, so . . .'

'It was good of you to risk your life to help us,' said Sarah.

He shrugged. 'Call it a sudden impulse. I haven't worried about anyone but myself for a very long time now – but when I saw you were in trouble, I just had to come and help.'

'I'm very glad you did, sir,' said Tom. 'I'm Tom Martin, and this is my cousin Sarah.'

'I'm Basil Overton – Professor Overton, actually, not that it means anything these days. You can call me Baz. Care for some lemonade?'

He rushed out of the room, returning with a big plastic bottle of lemonade and three glasses. 'Still a few bottles left,' he said. 'No ice, though, I'm afraid.'

He poured lemonade for Tom and Sarah and they drank thirstily.

Baz looked at them with shrewd, twinkling eyes. 'So what are you two young people up to?' he asked. 'Why didn't you know about the giant rats on the heath?'

'We've just come back to England,' said Sarah. 'From America.'

Which was true, more or less, she thought. They'd been coming back from New York when a malfunctioning transmat system had bounced them into a series of alternative universes.

'Came on a relief plane, I suppose,' said Baz. 'I thought they'd stopped all those. Why on earth did you come back?'

'We didn't realise how bad things were,' said Tom. 'And we've got family here.'

'Here in London?'

'Here in Hampstead, actually,' said Sarah. 'A house not far from here. We were trying to reach it when we ran into the rats.'

'Well, you must try again, when you've had a rest,' said Baz. 'Though I must warn you it's more than likely that your family have moved away or . . .'

His voice tailed off.

'Or that they're all dead,' said Sarah quietly.

'We're prepared for that,' said Tom. 'We just felt we had to go and see.'

Baz sighed. 'I lost my own family, you know,' he said. 'In the second plague. Somehow I didn't have the heart to move after that. Besides, I didn't want to leave the heath. I've always loved it, and even in its changed state it still fascinates me.'

'What's that weird stuff growing all over it?' asked Tom.

'And where did those horrible rats come from?' asked Sarah.

'It's a long story,' said Baz. 'And a very sad one. The weed and the rats and all the other horrors didn't really come from anywhere. We created them ourselves and turned them loose upon the world . . .'

'Who'd do a thing like that?' asked Tom. 'Baron Frankenstein?'

'Funny you should say that,' said Baz. 'People used to talk about Frankenstein foods . . .'

Tom and Sarah looked puzzled and Baz went on, 'It all started when we discovered genetic modification.'

'I've heard of that,' said Sarah. 'It was discovered towards the end of the twentieth century. Research into genetic modification was restricted and eventually banned altogether. Everyone decided it was just too dangerous.'

Tom shot her a warning glance. Sarah was talking of what had happened in *their* world. 'That may have happened in some places, Sarah. Perhaps things were different here.' He looked at Baz. 'I gather that here you just let things rip.'

'We certainly did,' said Baz bitterly. 'We discovered how to improve plants – and animals as well. We made sheep grow bigger, cows give more milk, pigs grow fatter than ever. We made wheat and all kinds of fruits and vegetables that resisted weedkillers and pesticides. Farmers could kill all the weeds and pests and not harm their crops.'

'Sounds fine to me,' said Tom. 'What's wrong with that?'

'Killing the pests meant the birds and small animals that lived on them had nothing to eat. Whole species died out.'

'It upset the balance of the ecosystem,' added Sarah.

Baz nodded. 'And even that wasn't the worst of it. Somehow the genetic improvements, the toughness and the increased resistance, got transmitted from the farm animals and the crops to some of the weeds and pests. We ended up with super-weeds that were virtually unkillable. Giant hogweed is one of the worst. It was always hard to get rid of it, now it's impossible. It's taken over the heath, taken over most of the country, and killed off everything else. The growth genes got transferred too. As well as giant sheep and pigs we got giant rats, bigger and fiercer than anyone had ever seen. I think they've probably eaten most of the other surviving animals. Now they're spreading all over the country – they're unstoppable as well.'

'Did this happen everywhere?' asked Sarah.

'Not in exactly the same way. But in one way or another, agriculture started to go wrong all over the world.' Baz sighed. 'I suppose we might still have sorted it out in the end. The trouble is that the global warming catastrophe came along at more or less the same time, one crisis on top of another. There were the climate changes, then the flooding and the plagues and all the other problems. The ecology crashed, civilisation collapsed – and we did it all ourselves!'

CHAPTER NINE

STRANGE HOMECOMING

TOM AND Sarah sat silently for a moment after Baz had finished his story.

The alternative-universe theory strikes again! thought Tom. Everything that went right in our world went wrong in this one.

With us, governments started worrying about pollution and global warming in plenty of time. Then transmat was invented and helped solve most of the problems.

Here, nobody worried about pollution until it was too late – and to make things worse the transmat experiments failed.

We put a stop to genetic modification experiments.

They went ahead with them and ended up ruining the ecology . . .

He could see that much the same thoughts were running through Sarah's mind.

'I couldn't help noticing you said "we" a lot,' she said quietly, 'when you were talking about the genetic modification experiments.'

Baz hesitated for a moment. Then he groaned. 'I suppose there's no point in trying to hide it now. Yes, heaven forgive me, I was one of the pioneer scientists in the field. Mind you, I meant well – not that that's any excuse. What's that old saying about good intentions?'

'The road to hell is paved with good intentions?' suggested Tom.

'That's the one,' said Baz. 'We took the road to hell all right. It was all so exciting at first, and it seemed to offer so many benefits. Super-crops and super-farm animals, lots of cheap food for everyone . . . It all happened so fast! Five years and everything was different. I did eventually realise that it was getting out of control, and I tried to warn everyone.'

'What happened?' asked Tom.

'I got fired,' said Baz simply. 'My research was declared valueless, I was accused of being an alarmist. By the time events proved I was right it was all too late.'

Baz sat staring into space. It was clear that he was thinking about his wife and children – the ones who'd died in one of the terrible plagues that followed the catastrophe.

Baz had paid a heavy price for his early lack of foresight – and so had everyone else for theirs.

Baz made an effort to cheer up. 'Let's have something to eat,' he suggested. 'Then we can go and try to find your family. I'll run you both round on the bike.'

Like the food they'd had with Jimmy, the meal Baz served came out of tins. They had tinned ham and tinned vegetables and tinned fruit. Baz even had a glass of wine with his meal.

'It's funny in a way,' he said. 'When agriculture collapsed people expected huge food shortages. But the plagues took care of that. There were so few left alive that there's still enough food left over to go round. Thousands – millions of people died. I was very ill for a long time myself after – after I lost my family. When I recovered I just hadn't the heart to move so I stayed on. Every now and again I go out and raid shops and stores and empty houses for supplies. Lots of places have already been looted, and sometimes it takes a long time but I always find something in the end. It's a scavenger's life . . .' He paused. 'I expect that, in the end, all the supplies will run out. But I don't suppose I'll be worried about it by then.'

When the meal was over, Baz stood up. 'Well, let's go and look for that family of yours.'

He got back into his motorcycle leathers and goggles and led them out of the flat and down to the garage.

Tom studied the tank and spray set-up that occupied most of the sidecar. 'What's in the tank?' he asked.

'It's a kind of knock-out gas in liquid suspension,' said Baz. 'My own invention! I got attacked again and again in the early days. Still do, occasionally, when I'm out scavenging. Sometimes by animals, like rats, or wild dogs or cats. Sometimes by humans – there are still a few bandits around.'

'We ran into some on the way,' said Tom. 'Sarah here scared them off with her Robin Hood act!'

'Good for her! Anyway, after a few narrow shaves I broke into a local lab and concocted this stuff. Some advantages in being a scientist after all!'

'Is it . . . fatal?' asked Sarah.

'No, but it causes instant unconsciousness,' said Baz cheerfully. 'Knocks out the attacker and gives me plenty of time to get away.'

In the back of the garage there was a big white Land Rover.

Tom studied it with keen interest.

Thanks to transmat, cars had survived only as a cult hobby in Tom and Sarah's world, like tractors and steam engines.

Sarah took no interest in them, happy to do all her travelling by transmat. Tom, however, was a keen steam and internal combustion fan. He had joined a club and learned to drive on one of the special private roads kept available for his fellow hobbyists.

'What a terrific car!' he said. 'Is that yours as well?'

'It is now,' said Baz. 'The former owner doesn't need it any more. I keep it filled up and in running order in case I want to make a long journey some time. But I never use it, to be honest, it's easier to get about on the motorbike, and it uses less petrol.'

'Where do you get your petrol?' asked Tom.

'Same as with food, I scavenge it where I can. There's still the odd can hidden here and there and I bring one home on the bike now and again. I've got quite a good stockpile now.'

He nodded to an array of cans stacked up against the rear wall of the garage.

Baz opened the garage doors, jumped on the bike and kicked it into life. 'Well, let's get going!'

He drove outside the garage and waited while Tom and Sarah closed the doors and climbed on to the sidecar, perching awkwardly on top of the gas tank.

Tom looked at Sarah and grinned. 'Hope it doesn't leak!'

'Where to?' asked Baz.

'Straight down the hill and turn right,' said Tom.

The motorbike zoomed away.

They sped down the hill in the middle of the road, keeping well clear of the thicket of giant hogweed that covered the road on either side. Sarah couldn't help fancying that malignant red eyes were watching her from the forest of green stalks.

Baz seemed to guess what she was thinking. 'Doesn't do to get too close,' he said. 'The rats don't usually bother you on the bike, they don't like the noise of the engine. But I had one jump right into the sidecar once.'

Sarah shuddered. 'What did you do?'

'I couldn't get at him with the spray, he was too close, so

I clobbered him with a spanner and chucked his body out for his mates.'

Tom and Sarah lived – or had lived in their own world – in one of the streets that ran between East Heath Road, which ran along the bottom of the hill, and the main High Street which ran along the top.

It was a narrow, steeply climbing street of tall old terraced houses, with flights of stone steps leading up to their front doors. It felt strange to be returning to it now, after so many adventures.

It was even stranger to be driving there perched on top of a tank of knock-out gas, driving through familiar streets now eerily silent and deserted.

'There it is!' said Tom, pointing. 'Number seven!'

Baz stopped the bike outside the house. 'You'll want to go in alone,' he said tactfully. 'I'll wait out here.'

Tom and Sarah climbed off the sidecar, went up to the front steps and stood looking up at the house where they'd both grown up.

'It looks the same – but different,' whispered Sarah. 'The front door's a different colour. Green, not blue.'

'Don't you remember?' said Tom. 'When we had the redecorating done? Mum wanted it green but Dad insisted on keeping the original blue!'

'Looks as if your mum won that one – here,' said Sarah. She hesitated. 'Tom, now we're here . . .'

'Do we really want to go in?' said Tom. 'I know. I was wondering that myself. If our this-world selves are in there and we meet them we'll be . . . *bounced*. Shot off to another universe like we were before.'

'We might end up in the right one,' said Sarah. 'Our own one, I mean. I think transmat is trying to get us back. We might actually get home, Tom.'

'We might,' said Tom. 'Or we might end up somewhere as strange as the SS World – or this one.'

Sarah nodded. 'I know. But we're going to risk it, aren't we?'

'Yes,' said Tom. 'I suppose we are.' He lowered his voice. 'Be a bit of a shock for old Baz if it happens!'

'And if they're not there,' said Sarah. 'If they've moved away, or if they're dead . . .'

'Then we try to find some scientist still working on transmat,' said Tom. 'Which means we go north . . .'

Baz was still watching them from his motorbike. 'What's up?' he called. 'Haven't you got keys?'

What had happened to their keys? wondered Tom. Left behind, somewhere in another universe. But he couldn't tell Baz that. 'We lost them in the floods,' he said.

Baz got off the bike and came to join them. 'Try knocking on the door,' he suggested practically. 'If there is anyone still there . . .'

'Right,' said Tom.

He and Sarah climbed the steps, side by side.

When they reached the front door, Tom looked at Sarah. 'Ready?'

'Ready!'

Tom reached out with his right hand and clasped Sarah's hand.

If they were about to be whizzed off to another universe, at least they'd arrive together.

He reached up and hammered on the front door.

CHAPTER TEN

DISCOVERY

THE SOUND of loud knocking echoed around the empty house and through the deserted street. Then it faded into silence.

There was no reply.

No alternate-universe Mum and Dad – or Tom and Sarah – opened the door.

Tom knocked again.

Still nobody came.

Baz cleared his throat. 'I don't want to sound discouraging,' he said awkwardly, 'but as I said, it's more than likely . . .' His voice tailed away.

'That they've either died or gone away?' said Tom. 'Yes, I know.'

He felt half disappointed, half relieved.

'Well, we'd better break in,' said Sarah.

Tom gave her a dubious look. 'Are you sure? We don't know what we might find in there.'

Sarah gave him a puzzled look and then realised what he was thinking. 'Oh yes, I see . . .'

There was at least a chance that the house might hold the dead bodies of their alternate-world parents. Or, worse still in a way, the bodies of their alternate-world selves.

Would the bodies have turned into skeletons by now?

And would the bouncing-on-to-another-dimension effect still work if you met yourself when you were dead? Would it work even if your other self was a skeleton?

Tom shuddered. He didn't much want to find out.

Baz's cheerful voice roused him from his gruesome thoughts. 'Here you go, then!'

He turned and saw that Baz was holding out a small mallet and a short, metal chisel.

'My burglar's kit,' said Baz. 'Never travel without it. Works fine on either doors or windows.'

Tom took the tools and looked at Sarah. 'Well?'

Sarah said, 'Go ahead. Whatever's in there, we need to know.'

Tom nodded. He put the sharp edge of the chisel between the edge of the door and the lock and bashed it in hard. Then he wrenched it sideways, and the lock gave way.

The door swung open.

Tom handed the tools back to Baz.

'You two go ahead,' said Baz. 'I'll keep watch out here just in case. If you need me, just yell.'

'Don't worry, we will!' said Tom. 'Come on, then, Sarah.'

They went into the hallway.

It was an eerie experience.

The layout of the house seemed to be unchanged.

Ground floor, spare room and parents' bedroom and bathroom – fortunately with no dead bodies.

First floor, kitchen and smaller sitting-room. The sitting-room seemed much the same but the kitchen was quite different.

'Looks like your mum got her new kitchen before things went wrong,' said Sarah.

'In our world they were still arguing about it,' said Tom. 'Dad kept saying it would be much too expensive. Mum insisted it would be an investment! I hope she got a bit of time to enjoy having it before . . .'

'Before they had to move,' said Sarah firmly. 'They're still alive, Tom, I'm sure of it.'

They went up another floor.

This held the big sitting-room, at the front of the house, and Tom's bedroom. He glanced quickly inside, and was glad to see that he wasn't already in there in the form of either corpse or skeleton.

The top floor held another bathroom, Sarah's bedroom, a small spare room – and Dad's study.

'The study's the place to look,' said Tom. 'Dad kept all the family papers and records there. Maybe we can find out what happened to them.'

'And us!' said Sarah.

They went into the big, book-lined room. It too

seemed much the same. There was the big desk, the computer work station, the filing cabinets . . .

Sarah looked round uneasily. 'It doesn't feel right, being in here. I keep expecting your dad to turn up and chase us off!'

'He was never very keen on visitors to his study, was he?' said Tom. 'We'd better have a look round all the same.'

'You do it,' said Sarah. 'He's your father. I'll take a look round the rest of the house – and I'd better go and tell Baz we're all right. Shan't be long.'

Sarah clattered off down the stairs.

Still half expecting an angry voice to bellow 'Tom! What do you think you're doing?' Tom opened his father's desk and began to search.

Sarah went to her own room first and found things largely unchanged. Her other self had a strange taste in CDs, though.

'Can't remember being an Oasis fan,' muttered Sarah.

Some of the clothes were pretty weird as well, but perhaps that was just alternate-world fashion.

She checked the cupboards and drawers and found them neat and tidy but largely empty. It looked as if her other self had packed up and gone away.

She went down to her uncle and aunt's room and found the same thing. But there was one very big difference.

Here the cupboards and drawers were standing open and things were in disarray, with clothes strewn on the bed and on the floor . . .

Sarah went back outside the house and found Baz sitting on his sidecar eating baked beans out of a can.

'Got to keep my strength up,' he said. 'Have a tin.'

Sarah opened a tin and Baz went on, 'Everything's quiet out here, nobody around. What's it like in the house?'

'Weird,' she replied. 'No dead bodies though, thank goodness. It looks as though they all moved away.'

'Any idea where to?'

'Not yet. Tom's searching for clues in his father's study . . .'

Sarah finished her baked beans and said, 'I'd better go and see how Tom's getting on.'

She went back into the house and ran up the stairs. She found Tom sitting at his father's desk with a litter of notebooks and papers in front of him.

He was staring into space with a sort of stunned look on his face. Sarah hoped he hadn't come across bad news.

'As far as I can see, everyone moved out some time ago,' she announced. 'I get the feeling we, the other us, went first in quite a leisurely, well-organised fashion. Later on your parents moved out too, only in much more of a hurry.'

Tom made no reply. He didn't even seem to hear her.

'Tom! Answer me. Did you find anything interesting in here?'

Tom gave her that same stunned look. 'Did I! Better prepare yourself for a surprise, Sarah!'

'Go on, then, amaze me!'

'Take a look around this study for a start. Do you see

anything different?'

Obediently, Sarah looked round. 'Not really,' she said after a moment. 'But I was never in here very much. Like you said, your dad didn't exactly encourage visitors when he was working.'

'Look at the books,' urged Tom.

Sarah looked. 'What about them? There were always books in here.'

'Not these ones. Look at the titles, the subjects.'

Sarah looked again. *Advanced Particle Physics*, *New Theories of Electro-Magnetic Radiation*, *Multiple Universe Theory* . . . They're all science books. High-powered ones, by the look of it.'

'That's right.'

'But your dad was a historian.'

'Right again.'

Sarah thought for a moment. 'But he was always interested in science, wasn't he? as a sort of hobby. I remember him telling me once, he was really keen on it at school. He only decided to do history at college at the last minute. It's the alternate-world thing again, Tom. In this world he must have stuck with science.'

'He certainly did,' said Tom. 'Take a look at this!' He handed her an open leather-bound volume. 'It's a kind of scrapbook.'

Sarah looked at the picture on the left-hand page. It showed two familiar figures in unfamiliar white coats, standing in front of a tangle of electronic equipment.

Sarah looked up. 'It's them! My uncle and aunt, your mum and dad.'

'Read the caption,' said Tom.

The caption under the picture read: *Professor Peter Martin and his wife Doctor Helena Martin, man-and-wife team of brilliant young scientists.* She looked up at him. 'Your this-world mum's a scientist too!'

'Now read the article,' said Tom. 'Go on, read it out loud, I want to hear it. I've read it three times but I still can't believe it myself!'

Sarah started reading out the article. '*Young Scientists still have Faith in Transmat* – that's the headline.'

'Go on!'

'*Professor Peter Martin, whose recent public experiment in matter transmission ended so disastrously, said this morning, "I can't deny that it was a big disappointment, but it wasn't entirely our fault. We were under great pressure to have the experiment ready for the exhibition in the Millennium Science Pavilion. Unfortunately we allowed ourselves to be rushed, and the experiment failed."*

'*His wife, Doctor Helena Martin, who collaborated with him on the experiments said, "We are both sure that transmat will ultimately work. It is vital that our experiments in matter transmission continue. Transmat holds the solution to many of the serious problems currently endangering our planet."*

'*It is rumoured however, that after the recent disaster, funding for transmat experiments is in grave danger of being cut off . . .*'

Sarah looked up from the scrapbook, her face as

astonished as Tom's had been. 'I don't believe it!'

'Neither did I, at first,' said Tom. 'But it's all down there. There's lots more stuff about it in the scrapbook as well. Not only did Mum and Dad become scientists in this world, they became the scientists who invented – or rather, failed to invent – transmat!'

CHAPTER ELEVEN

THE MESSAGE

TOM GAVE Sarah a moment to get over her shock. Then he picked up another book, its pages covered with sprawling writing.

'This is some kind of journal. It's hard to make out, but I managed to decipher a couple of the most important bits. Listen to this.'

Tom read out loud. '*We have decided to send Tom and Sarah to America while there is still time. In so huge a country the effects of the coming catastrophe may be less severe, and the Americans have greater scientific resources to counter it. We are sending them to my old friend Professor Hollister in Anchorage, Alaska. He too is working on matter transmission. Tom and Sarah are taking him copies of my notes which may assist him to carry on this vital work. We shall miss them very much but we are convinced that it is the best thing to do.*'

Tom turned to the end of the journal. 'This is the final entry.

'*Things are very bad here now. The climate seems to have undergone permanent change, flooding is on the increase and plague after plague is sweeping through the area. In London at least the final breakdown cannot be far away. The anti-scientist feeling among the survivors grows stronger every day. Friends and colleagues have been attacked, imprisoned and even killed, and it is no longer safe for us to stay. Fortunately, this emergency has long been foreseen by the scientific community, and we are going to the particular place that has been prepared for us – we are going north – "Over the seas" as the old song has it. There a few of us hope to preserve some vestige of science and civilisation . . .*'

Tom looked up. 'There's a kind of postscript. It's addressed to us.'

'To us?'

'Well, you know what I mean. The other us.'

He read out loud again: '*To Tom and Sarah: We have tried to reach you in America without success. Communication with the rest of the world seems to have broken down. I hope you will never read these words, that you are still safe and well in America. But if by any chance you should come back here and find us gone, I urge you to follow us north "Over the sea" to the place you know of, if you possibly can. I have every faith in your courage and resourcefulness, and our greatest hope is that some day , one way or another, we shall see you both again.*'

Tom closed the book. 'It's weird, isn't it? I know it's not really a message to us but . . .'

'I know,' said Sarah. 'It feels like one. And I think we'd

better act as if it was!'

'Suppose our this-world selves were here before us, and got the message?'

Sarah considered. 'I doubt it, I think they'd have taken the journal. We'll just have to risk it and go.'

'Go where? North? "Over the sea", whatever that means, wherever that is? Does he mean they're going abroad, somewhere? The Continent? Things must be just as bad there, what would be the point?'

'He said, *"Over the sea" as the song has it,*' said Sarah. 'But what song?'

Suddenly Tom jumped up. 'Of course, that's it! It's an old Scottish ballad, about the escape of Bonnie Prince Charlie after the Jacobite rebellion! That's where he escaped to – "Over the sea to Skye!" '

'Then that's where they've gone!' said Sarah. 'It all fits. Skye! An island off the coast of Scotland, about as far north as you can get!'

'I think you're right,' said Tom. 'We should go there as well. Maybe they can help us to get back home. Even if they can't, an alternate family is better than none!' He stood up. 'We'd better go. Baz will be getting worried.' He put the journal and the scrapbook back on the desk. 'We'll leave these here – just in case the this-world Tom and Sarah turn up after all . . .'

Outside the house they gave the patiently-waiting Baz an edited account of what they had found. They left out the whole alternate-world complication and simply told him they'd found a message from their parents asking them to join them in the north.

'So what are you going to do?' asked Baz.

'Go and find them,' said Sarah.

Baz nodded thoughtfully. 'It's a heck of a long way . . .'

He drove them back to his block of flats and parked inside the garage. He got off the motorbike and stood lost in thought for a moment. Tom and Sarah watched him, wondering what was going on.

Suddenly Baz said, 'Either of you drive?'

'I do,' said Tom.

Baz waved towards the big white Land Rover. 'Take her!'

Sarah stared at him. 'What do you mean?'

'Take the Land Rover,' said Baz. 'For your journey north.'

'We can't do that!' said Tom.

'You've got to,' said Baz. 'It'll take you for ever to do it on foot. You probably wouldn't survive.'

'We can't possibly take your car,' said Sarah.

'We'll do what you did,' said Tom. 'Find a car of our own.'

'You'll have a job,' said Baz. 'I got hold of this one ages ago. There's not much that's roadworthy left by now. Anyway, it'd take ages for you to find one, and ages more to stock it up with fuel and supplies. Why go through all that when it's all here for you?'

'But it's *yours*,' said Tom.

Baz grinned. 'Well, not really! Come upstairs and we'll talk it over.'

Back in his top-floor flat, Baz produced more lemonade for Tom and Sarah and poured himself a glass of wine. 'Listen,' he said. 'I'm never going anywhere in that Land Rover. It's just a kind of fantasy that one day I'll move away. I've got the motorbike for my little foraging trips and that's all I need.'

'Suppose you change your mind?' asked Sarah.

Baz shook his head. 'I won't, not now. I haven't the heart. I'm too old, too tired. I've got used to it here. No, you take her and welcome. I'll give you all the food and petrol I can spare. Enough to get you there with any luck.'

They argued with him for ages but he just wouldn't listen.

'Why don't you come with us, then?' suggested Tom.

For a moment Baz looked tempted, then he shook his head.

'Why not?' asked Sarah.

Baz led them over to the window and pointed to the garden down below. In a little patch of garden, kept clear from the giant weeds, they saw a white cross, flanked by two smaller ones.

Sarah said, 'Is that . . . ?'

Baz nodded. 'I buried them there myself. I had to, the cemeteries were all full. I don't want to leave them now.'

There didn't seem any point in arguing after that.

'Cheer up,' said Baz. 'I'll be fine. Stay here tonight and we'll have a farewell dinner. Then you can make an early start in the morning!'

They spent the rest of the day loading the big Land Rover with cans of petrol and stores of food. In spite of their protests Baz insisted on them taking as much as the vehicle could carry.

When the Land Rover was loaded up, they went out for a trial run so that Tom could get used to the big car. Despite its size, power steering made it surprisingly easy to handle.

That night they had another all-tinned feast – chicken, potatoes, peas and suet pudding.

After dinner Baz produced maps and went over the route with them.

'I don't really know what conditions are like further north,' he said. 'There's no guarantee you won't run into some kind of trouble. More flooding maybe . . . But if you can I'd just stick to the motorway and put your foot down . . . Motorways are boring, but they're efficient.' He yawned. 'We'd better get some sleep. I'll see you to the beginning of the motorway anyway. After that, you're on your own.'

Next morning early they set off. The sky was still dark and sullen, and there were occasional patches of acrid mist, but there was at least a hint of sunshine behind the clouds.

Baz led the way on his motorbike, guiding them

through the tangle of the ruined North Circular to the place where the motorway began.

They stopped and looked at the wide stretch of roadway ahead.

It was cracked and broken in places, and there was rubble of one kind and another scattered over it, and even the occasional abandoned or burnt-out car. It looked cluttered and messy. But it didn't look impassable.

'It'll take you two days, maybe three, depending on conditions,' said Baz. 'If I were you I'd park somewhere safe-looking and sleep in the car. Take it in turns to keep watch.'

He rooted inside his saddlebag. 'You'd better take this.'

He produced a shotgun and handed it over. 'Know how to use it?'

Tom shook his head. 'Not really.'

Baz fished out a box of cartridges. 'You break the gun – like this – put a cartridge in each barrel, and snap the gun shut. Couldn't be simpler.'

He made them both practise till they got it right.

Sarah wasn't happy about it. 'We're not planning on shooting anyone,' she said.

'It's only bird-shot,' said Baz. 'You won't hurt anyone very badly unless they're close – and if they're not close you won't hit them anyway. But you might find it useful against the rats.'

Sarah looked alarmed. 'You mean they're not just on the heath?'

Baz shook his head. 'I told you, they've spread all over the country. They've settled in colonies in the giant hogweed – and they'll attack anything edible that enters their territory.'

He patted the shotgun and handed it over to Tom. 'It'll make a useful addition to your bow and arrow, Sarah! Well, good luck!'

Tom took the shotgun and tucked it between the front seats. He leaned out of the window and shook hands.

'I won't try to thank you,' he said. 'You've been more generous than I can say.'

'Goodbye, Baz,' said Sarah. 'We can't thank you enough.'

Baz adjusted his goggles, touched his helmet in salute, wheeled the bike around and zoomed back the way they'd come.

Tom looked at the long empty motorway stretching ahead. 'Right!' he said determinedly. 'Next stop Scotland.'

He started the engine and the big Land Rover roared away.

CHAPTER TWELVE

NORTHBOUND

IT WAS exciting at first, zooming along the empty motorway in the big white Land Rover.

Tom loved driving and in his own world he'd been restricted to a few circuits around a private track. He was looking forward to doing a really long drive for once.

Except for a brief journey with Tom in the SS World, Sarah had scarcely travelled by car at all. Like all her generation she was used to going everywhere by transmat.

You got in a transmat booth at your starting point, dialled your destination, and stepped out of a booth wherever you wanted to be. So the journey by road was a novelty for her as well.

They sped along the long straight motorway, swerving occasionally to avoid lumps of rubble, bits of torn-up road and the occasional rusting and deserted vehicle.

'I wonder what happened to their owners?' said Sarah.

'Maybe they just ran out of fuel,' said Tom.

They passed a wrecked car with a grinning skeleton at the wheel.

'Or out of luck,' added Tom grimly. 'We must stay alert, Sarah.'

Sarah nodded. 'I'm sure you're right. But alert for what? At the moment there doesn't seem to be a soul around.'

'Something will happen sooner or later,' said Tom. 'It always does!'

The journey went on – and on and on.

Once there was a sudden violent rainstorm, like the one they'd seen in London. It was impossible to drive in it – windscreen wipers just couldn't cope and you couldn't see a thing. The only thing to do was to sit and wait it out, with the rain drumming down on the Land Rover's roof.

The storm came to an end at last, and they drove on.

Suddenly there was a patch of blindingly bright sunshine. It lasted for about half an hour. Then it rained again, but not so hard.

Not long after that they had to crawl through a thick belt of mist.

At one point a stream of water flowed across the motorway.

Tom gritted his teeth and put his foot down, hoping desperately that the car engine wouldn't be flooded. All he knew about cars was how to drive them. If they had a breakdown, he'd be helpless.

Luckily the water was only about ten centimetres deep and the big Land Rover coped with it without trouble.

Unlike the weather, the scene on the motorway didn't change – road, rubble, wrecked cars.

From time to time footbridges arced over the motorway. Quite a few had wrecked cars underneath them, but the footbridges were all deserted.

And there was nothing much to look at in the way of scenery either.

The first part of their journey they were passing by silent, deserted cities.

As they came out into open country, they passed between fields, all overgrown with giant hogweed, or with some other strange-looking crop. Mostly the fields were dull green. Occasionally they were bright yellow.

'I think the yellow stuff's called rape,' said Sarah. 'They used to grow it for the oil. I suppose it just mutated, like the hogweed, and drove out everything else. So, no food crops, no farm animals. No wonder everything collapsed.'

Every now and again they passed roadside buildings, all with shattered windows and doors broken open.

'Motorway service stations,' said Tom. 'Baz told me about them. There were cafés and shops and places to buy petrol. Looks like they all got looted ages ago.'

They drove on and on. Some of the roadside motorway signs had been wrecked, and some of the overhead ones had crashed down into the road, but there were enough left to tell them they were still on the right road.

'Baz was right,' said Tom after a while.

'About what?'

'Motorways are boring, but efficient. Basically there's just one big straight road that goes most of the way to Scotland.'

'He was right about the boring bit,' said Sarah.

'The trouble is, we've both been spoiled by transmat. It's made us forget what a lot of space there is between different places!'

'It wouldn't be so bad if there was something to look at,' said Sarah. 'It's all so – sameish! And no people!'

'That may be just as well,' said Tom. 'Some of the people we've met so far haven't been all that friendly.'

'There was Jimmy, in the store,' said Sarah. 'And Baz. I think we've been very lucky . . .' Suddenly she pointed. 'Look, there are some people, up ahead. On that footbridge by that service station . . .'

A little group of people stood on the footbridge ahead, waving frantically.

'Shall we stop?' asked Sarah. 'Maybe they can tell us something useful about conditions ahead.'

Tom shook his head. 'We'll wave back and keep right on going.'

'But they may be in trouble!'

'If we stop, we may be in trouble.'

Tom frowned, peering at the scattering of wrecked cars ahead. As they came up to the bridge he suddenly swung the Land Rover in a huge curve, passing under the bridge on the far side of the road. A massive chunk of rubble crashed down from the bridge, missing them by centimetres.

Tom straightened out the Land Rover, stepped on the accelerator and drove on.

Sarah looked back at the people on the bridge, who were now yelling and shaking their fists in anger.

'Stupid murderous vandals!' she said indignantly. 'You think people would have better things to do when things are like this. They could have killed us.'

'They were *trying* to kill us,' said Tom. 'They weren't vandals, they were bandits. They throw chunks of rubble down to wreck any passing cars, then come down and loot them.'

'How did you know what was going to happen?'

'I noticed that under nearly all of those footbridges there were more chunks of rubble than usual about – and more wrecked cars. Sometimes it pays to have a suspicious mind!'

'They can't do very well at it,' said Sarah. 'Apart from us, there aren't any other cars to attack.'

'What you might call a dying business,' agreed Tom.

They drove on.

Eventually Sarah dropped off to sleep, and after several more hours of driving, Tom found his head starting to nod as well. Even without any other traffic on the road this was a dangerous situation. He didn't want to nod off and crash the car.

He stopped the car on a deserted stretch of motorway, got out and stood in the roadway, yawning and stretching.

Sarah woke up and got out of the car as well.

'Sorry, I just nodded off.'

'I nearly did myself,' said Tom. 'You know, I'm rapidly losing my love of old-fashioned internal combustion travel. The sooner we get back to a world with transmat the better!'

He looked up and down the endless motorway. 'They had things called traffic jams in the old days, I've seen it in historical films. Imagine travelling like this in a mass of other cars, all yelling and hooting.'

'All sending out clouds of pollution as well,' said Sarah. 'Cars had a lot to do with the state this world's in now. They accounted for a lot of the pollution, the pollution helped to damage the ozone layer and caused global warming, the global warming caused the flooding . . .'

'Let's hope my alternative dad is getting on well with his transmat experiments,' said Tom.

They drove on again, stopping for a rest and a snack whenever Tom felt too tired to drive. Finally he pulled up in one of the bays by the side of the road.

'That's it, I can't keep my eyes open. And it's starting to get dark as well. We'll stop here for the night.'

Sarah looked up and down the bleak stretch of road. 'Here?'

'Why not? It's as good as anywhere.'

'We could go on to one of those service station places. Some of them had signs with beds on.'

'Too dangerous,' said Tom. 'Remember our rubble-chucking friends? We met them just by a service station. I reckon those places will have been taken over by local gangs. We'll do better to sleep in the car – we've got food and drink and everything we need. You can have the back seat and I'll take the front.'

'You're probably right,' said Sarah. 'Let's have some supper.'

Baz had been generous with his supplies and they had a meal of tinned beans and tinned sausages, followed by tinned peaches and washed down with cans of Coke.

'How far have we come?' asked Sarah.

Tom looked at one of the maps Baz had provided. 'According to that last sign we saw, we're somewhere near Sheffield. I make that about a third of the way.'

Sarah nodded. 'Didn't Baz say it'd take about three days? We're not doing too badly.'

'I'll take first watch,' said Tom. 'I'll wake you in a few hours and you can take over.'

They finished their meal and Sarah settled down to sleep.

She curled up under a blanket in the roomy back seat and went off to sleep almost at once. Tom could hear her gently snoring. He grinned, knowing she'd deny it furiously in the morning.

Tom stretched out in the front passenger seat with the shotgun on his lap. He was very tired, but he was determined to keep awake. It wasn't easy.

Every now and again his head nodded, he closed his eyes and he saw an unending ribbon of motorway unreeling itself in front of him . . .

He was beginning to drift off to sleep without realising, when he heard a faint but distinct rattling sound.

Someone was trying to open the Land Rover door . . .

CHAPTER THIRTEEN

THE BARRIER

TOM FROZE, wondering what to do next.

I'll start the car! he thought. Just start the car and drive off! I don't know who's out there, and I don't want to know.

Still clutching the shotgun he slid across into the driving seat and reached for the ignition key.

Just as his fingers touched the key, the front passenger door swung open. Despairingly Tom realised he'd forgotten to lock it.

He peered out into the darkness and saw a swarm of dark shapes huddled around the car.

Dark, furry shapes with gleaming red eyes and yellow fangs.

The attackers weren't human, they were rats. Giant rats, like the ones they'd seen on the heath.

The rat that had opened the door, a huge creature even larger than the others, was crouched up on its haunches, poised to spring . . .

As the giant rat leaped for his throat, Tom raised Baz's shotgun and blasted it away.

Sarah woke with a yell of alarm.

Tom fired the second barrel into the seething crowd of rats, slammed the door shut again, locked it, and started the Land Rover.

They shot forwards, bumping over shapes that squealed and died beneath the wheels. Tom gritted his teeth and put his foot down. The bumps and squeals were left behind and the Land Rover sped on.

'Hey, what's going on?' yelled Sarah from the back seat.

'Oh nothing,' said Tom airily. He was feeling almost hysterical with sheer relief. 'Just thought I'd get a bit of an early start. Some friends gave me a wake-up call!'

'Tom, tell me what happened!'

Tom told her about the rats. 'I'm sorry, Sarah, it's all my fault. I fell asleep on duty.'

'A rat opened the car door?' said Sarah incredulously.

'Like a fool, I forgot to lock it. Mind you it would probably have just picked the lock even if I had. They must have giant brains as well. I expect they'll take over the planet eventually.'

'What made them attack us like that?'

'I imagine they smelled food and came to find it.'

'The supplies, you mean?'

'The supplies and us,' said Tom grimly. 'They're not too fussy about their diet. Remember that skeleton we saw back in the car?'

They drove on till they felt they'd put a safe distance between themselves and the rats, then stopped for a hasty breakfast and a wash in mineral water.

Then Sarah got in the front of the car, the reloaded shotgun on her lap, while Tom got some sleep in the back seat.

A few hours later he awoke refreshed and they drove on – and on and on.

The rest of the day didn't live up to its exciting start. They just kept driving, stopping occasionally for a rest and a snack, and then going on their way.

'This is getting monotonous,' complained Sarah. 'Not that I want more bandits or another rat attack . . . But it would be nice if something happened.'

'I wouldn't complain if I were you,' said Tom. 'Remember the old Chinese curse?'

'What old Chinese curse?'

'It goes, "May you live in interesting times,"' said Tom. 'Things have been far too interesting recently! Anyway, we'll be stopping for the night soon.'

'How far have we got now then?'

'We're coming up to Newcastle and that's right on the border with Scotland.'

'I'm glad to hear it,' said Sarah. 'I don't think I can take much more motorway.'

'It'll be different tomorrow,' said Tom consolingly. 'We come off the motorway around Newcastle and the going may be a bit trickier. We'll be driving through some pretty wild country to reach Skye.'

'Country that's been wild all along may be safer than places that used to be civilised and have gone wild,' said Sarah. 'As I remember, lots of Scotland was always pretty empty.'

Tom peered ahead. 'Full or empty, it looks like we may never get the chance to find out. Someone seems to have rebuilt Hadrian's Wall.'

In the distance, some way ahead of them, a roughly-built barrier stretched right across the motorway. It was made from chunks of rubble, wrecked cars and huge blocks of stone.

Tom looked at Sarah. 'What do we do now? I could put my foot down and crash through it.'

'I'm not so sure,' said Sarah. 'It's crude, but it looks pretty solid. We don't want to smash up the Land Rover.'

'We don't want to drive into a bandit ambush either,' Tom pointed out. 'I'll turn the Land Rover before we get to it and we'll go back.'

'Back to London?'

'No, of course not. I'm not suggesting we give up. We can take one of the motorway exits, try to work our way around the barrier.'

'I'm not sure it is bandits,' said Sarah thoughtfully. 'I just can't see bandits building an elaborate barrier like that.'

'Why not? If they want to stop people and rob them . . .'

'A lot of effort went into putting up that barrier. I don't see bandits taking the trouble. Wave a knife at you, or chuck a lump of rubble, that's more their style. Something like that barrier suggests organisation. If there is any sort of civilisation up here, this may be the first sign of it.'

'Well, it doesn't look too friendly,' grumbled Tom. 'All right, I'll drive up to it slowly and see what kind of reception we get.'

As they drove closer to the barrier, they could see that there was a gap in the centre, barred by a big wooden gate. The gate was guarded by two roughly-dressed men carrying spears.

One of them was grim and sour-faced with a short black beard.

The other was fat and spotty with flaming ginger hair.

They were both very large and hairy and looked extremely unfriendly.

Tom stopped the car a little way from the gate. He wound the window right down and put his head out. 'Could you let us through, please?' he asked politely.

One of the men said gruffly, 'Who are you? What's your business here?'

'We've got family in Scotland,' said Tom. 'We're trying to reach them.'

'Family? Where?'

His lingering suspicions made Tom give a cautious reply. 'We're not sure. We only know they're in Scotland somewhere.'

'You don't come from round here,' said the red-haired man accusingly.

'No, we don't. Our parents came up here when the trouble started.'

'More damned refugees,' said the first man. 'Coming up here scrounging our food. Now their brats are following them up here as well. Send them back.'

'Please, listen,' said Sarah.

The sour-faced man said, 'Shut your mouth, girl, when men are talking.'

That did it. Sarah had a pretty short fuse at the best of times. Now, tired and frazzled, she was just about ready to snap. Before Tom could stop her, she threw open her door, jumped out of the car and marched up to the two men.

'Now listen, you two Neanderthals,' she said indignantly. 'We're not refugees, and we're not scrounging either. We've brought our own supplies. It's vitally important that we find our family. Now, will you please open that gate and let us through!'

Tom groaned. He'd been trying to keep things low-key and friendly, but Sarah's angry tone was having the opposite effect.

'I told you to shut your mouth, girl!' snarled the sour man. 'We decide who gets through this gate and who doesn't – and you don't! Clear off, the both of you!'

The man's tone of contemptuous dismissal was just too much. 'Open this gate!' Sarah yelled. 'Or do I have to open it myself?'

She marched up to the gate and started shoving it open. The fat, red-haired man grabbed her arm with one huge hand and dragged her away.

'Let me go!' yelled Sarah. Swinging her fist in an upward loop, she delivered a savage box on the ear. With a yell of pain, the ginger-haired man raised his other fist for a blow that would have flattened her.

Tom grabbed the shotgun, stuck it out of the open window and fired one barrel in the air.

The boom of the shotgun sounded tremendously loud and the two guards froze.

Tom broke open the gun, fed in a cartridge and snapped it closed again. He trained the shotgun on the two men.

'Let her go!' he ordered. 'Let her go and open the gate!'

The man holding Sarah released her and she ran back to the Land Rover and got in.

'Now open the gate,' repeated Tom. 'And get a move on. This thing's got two barrels and they're both loaded . . .'

The two guards glared fiercely at him. For a moment Tom was afraid they'd call his bluff.

The first one said, 'Let them through. They won't get far.'

The two men shoved the gate open.

Tom drove swiftly through and zoomed away.

One of the men ran to a crude signalling device at the side of the road and jerked on a rope. On top of the tall pole the signal began wagging to and fro . . .

CAPTURED

SARAH WAS still seething as they drove away from the barrier.

'Of all the nerve! A couple of spear-carrying thugs, setting up barriers, telling people where they can and can't go . . . Still, we showed them.'

Tom sighed.

The trouble was, Sarah had grown up in a free society, where the rights of the individual were sacred. She just wasn't used to being bossed about by petty authority.

Or to being told to shut up when the men were talking either. That had probably been the proverbial last straw!

'Things may be about to start getting a bit tricky, Sarah,' he said.

'What do you mean?'

'You said yourself, that barrier meant some sort of organisation. Those spear-carrying thugs may represent the law round here.'

'So?'

'Well, if they do represent the law, we've just broken it!'

Sarah was silent for a moment. 'You're right,' she said. 'Sorry! It was just the way they treated us. And when one of them grabbed my arm like that – I just lost it!'

'And struck a blow for women's liberation – literally!'

'What do you think will happen?'

'I don't know if you noticed but they had a signalling set-up back there. It's possible someone will come after us. I expect they sent out some sort of general alarm. For all I know, we are now the Bonnie and Clyde of the border country!'

'Who?'

'Bonnie and Clyde,' repeated Tom. 'A couple of gun-crazy outlaws in an old twentieth-century movie.'

'What about them?'

'They defied the law and died in a hail of bullets!'

Sarah winced. 'Ouch! I really am sorry, Tom.'

'I'm as bad as you are,' said Tom. 'Worse – I fired the shotgun. It was the only way I could see to stop you getting your head knocked off!' He grinned wryly. 'No point in agonising about it, it's done now.'

'What are we going to do?'

Tom considered. 'We're off the motorway, so maybe we can get away on to some minor road, hide in the hills somewhere.'

'There's a crossroads up ahead,' said Sarah. 'And a sign, I think. I'll take a look at the map.'

She bent her head over the map. Tom tapped her on the shoulder. 'Don't bother,' he said grimly.

'Why not?'

'Look!'

A group of men were moving a barrier across the road ahead. Tom glanced quickly over his shoulder. If he could double back . . .

To his astonishment, he saw a jeep pull out of a sideroad and fall in behind them. It was full of armed men.

They were trapped.

Sarah took in the situation. 'Can we crash the barrier?'

Tom shook his head. 'Not this time. We're outnumbered and outgunned, we'd only get ourselves killed.' He gave her a reassuring grin. 'We'll just have to try and talk ourselves out of trouble. Just stay cool this time, Sarah, and try not to hit anyone! A lot of those men have got guns, and they don't look very pleased. The only hopeful thing about this situation is, I think you were right about the barrier. Guards, a signalling system, and now a mobile patrol. It all looks like an official set-up to me.'

'What's good about that?'

'At least it's better than bandits. They'll probably give us a trial before they shoot us.'

'Terrific!'

'Seriously though, Sarah, play it cool. The main thing now is not to get ourselves shot by accident.'

Tom slowed down the Land Rover and drove up to the barrier. The men guarding it wore a scrappy assortment of uniforms, and they all had armbands with a black eagle symbol on them.

Unlike the spear-carrying guards these men all had guns – shotguns and sporting rifles mostly. Tom guessed they must be some sort of special patrol group.

The guns were all pointing at Tom and Sarah.

Tom reached for the shotgun to hand it over.

'Better not touch it,' said Sarah. 'Just get out and tell them where it is.'

Tom realised she was right. In a tense situation like this, reaching for a gun – for any reason – could get you killed.

Tom drew the car to a halt and sat quietly, waiting.

The jeep pulled up behind them, and four men, armed and uniformed like the ones at the barrier, jumped out and surrounded the Land Rover.

Their leader was a very tall, black-haired man with a heavy moustache.

Sergeant's stripes were sewn to the sleeves of his green waxed jacket, and he wore a holstered revolver on his belt.

He had a deep, commanding voice. 'Everybody keep calm. No need for anyone to get hurt.'

It was quite clear that his words were addressed as much to his own men as to Tom and Sarah. The little group of guards was excited, angry and armed – a dangerous combination.

Tom wound down the window. 'It's all right,' he called. 'We won't give you any trouble.'

'Get out of the car, nice and slowly, and raise your hands,' ordered the sergeant.

Tom looked at Sarah. 'Let's just do exactly as he says. All right?'

'Don't worry. I've had my violent outburst for the day!'

They got out of the car and raised their hands.

'Where are your weapons?' demanded the sergeant.

'There's a loaded shotgun in the front between the seats,' said Tom.

'And a bow and some arrows in the back,' said Sarah.

The sergeant nodded to a couple of his men and they took the shotgun and the bow from out of the car.

'Any other weapons?'

'I've got a Swiss Army knife in my pocket.'

'Take it out, please, slowly, and hand it over.'

Tom obeyed.

The sergeant looked at them. 'Is this the lot of you?'

Tom nodded towards the Land Rover, now being searched by a couple of the sergeant's men. 'You can see for yourself – there's only us.'

The sergeant shook his head wonderingly. 'A couple of kids! The way I heard it, we were being invaded by the English army – or at the very least an assault by a heavily armed gang of border bandits!' He raised his voice. 'All right, lads, relax, I think we can handle these two dangerous outlaws between the lot of us!'

There was a chuckle, and to Tom's relief most of the threatening guns were lowered.

'All right,' said the sergeant again. 'What happened?'

They told the same story they'd told at the first barrier – they'd come north in search of their family.

'So how did it end in shooting at the border guards?' asked the sergeant.

'That was my fault,' said Sarah. 'Your border guards were pretty rude and I lost my temper. One of them grabbed my arm and I thumped him.'

'Did you now? Which one did you thump?'

'The fat one with red hair.'

There was another chuckle from the now fascinated audience.

'That'll teach Fat Hamish to mind his manners!'

When the laughter had died down the sergeant said, 'And the shooting?'

'That was me,' said Tom. 'Fat Hamish was about to bash her back – and he's a lot bigger than she is. So I fired a shot in the air to warn him off. Then I made them open the gate – and here we are.'

'So you are,' said the sergeant. 'The question is, what do I do with you?'

Sarah gave him her most winning smile. 'Can't you just let us go on our way? I'm really sorry I hit your guard but he attacked me first.'

'I'm afraid I can't do that,' said the sergeant. 'Armed attack on a border guard is a serious matter.' He considered for a moment. 'There's only one thing for it. I'll have to take the both of you before the High Provost.'

'Who's he?' asked Tom.

'He's the man in charge. Here, and for a very long way around here.'

'And where is he now?' asked Sarah.

The sergeant gave her a look of surprise. 'In Edinburgh, of course. Where else?' He considered for a moment. 'Andy, give me that shotgun. You lads, move that barrier.' He turned to Tom and Sarah. 'You two, get back in the Land Rover. I'll ride in the back seat, just follow my directions.'

One of the men called, 'Hadn't we all better come with you, sergeant? Yon's a very dangerous female!'

'Ask Fat Hamish!' said someone else.

There was a roar of laughter.

Clearly, thought Tom, Sarah had picked exactly the right guard to thump.

Ignoring his men, the sergeant climbed into the back seat. In a surprisingly short time they were on their way again.

Only now they were prisoners.

They rode in a tense silence for the first part of the journey.

Sarah gave Tom an enquiring look. Were they going to try to escape?

Tom gave a tiny shake of his head and Sarah frowned.

The sergeant seemed to guess their thoughts. 'Listen, you two, just don't give me any trouble, all right? I've got kids your age, and I don't want to hurt you. I'm bigger than both of you put together, I've got your shotgun and my own revolver. I used to be a gamekeeper and I'm a very good shot. Even if you did manage to overpower me and get away, there's a message been sent ahead and the checkpoint guards will be looking out for us. If we miss one, they'll all be out hunting for you.'

'All right,' said Tom calmly.

'Why don't you both give me your parole?' suggested the sergeant.

Tom looked puzzled. 'My what?'

'Your word of honour not to try to escape. Then we can all enjoy the drive.'

'All right,' said Tom. 'I'll give you my parole as far as Edinburgh.'

Sarah gave him a surprised look.

'We're travelling in the direction we want to go, anyway,' Tom went on. 'We might as well do it with you as a guide.'

'Fair enough,' said the sergeant. 'And does that go for you as well, young lady? Like my men say, it seems you're the dangerous one!'

Sarah laughed. 'All right. Sergeant, I give you my parole. You're safe till Edinburgh.'

They drove on their way, this time through narrower, more winding roads. Every now and again they passed a guarded checkpoint.

Each time the sergeant signalled, and the guard waved them on.

'What's this High Provost like?' asked Sarah after a while.

'He's a hard man,' said the sergeant. 'Hard but fair. You'll get a chance to tell him your side of the story. For your sake, I just hope he believes it!'

CHAPTER FIFTEEN

THE HIGH PROVOST

IT WAS late afternoon by the time they reached Edinburgh. As they drove along Princes Street, past Edinburgh Castle on its hill, they were surprised how normal everything looked compared to the devastated London they had left behind.

There were people on the streets and some of the shops were open. There was even a little traffic – quite a few bicycles and the odd car.

Sarah remarked on it to the sergeant.

'Things are getting better,' he said. 'Mind you, they were bad at first. Very bad for a while. But we were never so industrialised as down south, so the collapse didn't hit us so hard.'

'What about the flooding?' asked Tom.

'We had a fair bit of that – most of the harbour area's gone. We had the bad weather too – but it wasn't nearly so extreme. Besides, we're used to it up here. The worst thing was the plagues – brought up here by refugees from the south. Luckily they seem to have burned out, but the memory lingers. We had a small population to begin with, and it's tiny now.'

'All the same,' said Tom, 'it's astonishing how much better things are up here.'

Now that they'd both given him their parole, the sergeant seemed relaxed and ready to talk. 'There are reasons for that,' he said. 'The floods and storms, all the global warming problems were much worse in the southern areas. As I say, we got off lightly up here, compared to the south and west.'

'What about all the problems with genetically modified foods and animals?' asked Sarah.

'We had no truck with that nonsense! We had our independence by the millennium, and our Scottish parliament passed strict laws against it.'

'Didn't the mutations from the south spread up here?' asked Tom.

'They did,' said the sergeant grimly. 'Lots of our crops and animals were infected – but not all of them. We can still grow food, and we have some healthy cattle and sheep – and the deer.'

It was obvious that smaller, more scattered communities, used to looking after themselves, had coped better with the ecological disasters than the crowded cities of the south.

'I'm afraid quite a few of our worst troubles came from

the south,' the sergeant went on. 'When they heard things were better up here, a lot of your bandits came raiding.'

'Hence the border guards,' said Tom.

The sergeant nodded. 'Things were bad for a while. And of course we had villains of our own keen to profit from the troubles. There was a breakdown in law and order for a time, but that's mostly over now. Except for the coastal pirates.'

'Pirates?' asked Sarah incredulously.

'Well, not real pirates. Sea thieves. They creep round the coast in their boats, and raid little settlements and villages.'

The sergeant peered out of the window. 'Well, we've arrived at last.'

The High Provost's house was in New Town – which was actually an area of splendid old houses built in the eighteenth century.

Following the sergeant's directions, Tom drove up to one of the largest and most magnificent of them and parked in the driveway outside. The sergeant led them up a small flight of steps to a splendid front door. He knocked and a white-haired old lady in a black dress opened the door.

'Come in, come in, Sergeant Mackenzie,' she said. 'The High Provost is expecting you.'

She ushered them into a gloomy, oak-panelled hall.

'These young people could do with some refreshment, Morag,' said Sergeant Mackenzie. He looked sternly at

Tom and Sarah. 'Must I send for a guard, or are you still on parole?'

'We'll extend our paroles for the rest of the day if you like,' said Tom. He suddenly realised he was very hungry.

Sergeant Mackenzie nodded and disappeared up some stairs. Morag took them both downstairs into a huge, old-fashioned, stone-flagged kitchen and gave them a bowl of delicious stew and chunks of home-made bread.

'Eat up, my dears,' she said.

'What is it?' asked Sarah.

'It's venison, child, very good for you. It'll build up your strength.'

Sarah was so hungry that she overcame her scruples and ate two bowls.

Tom ate three.

There was fruitcake to follow and they were sitting back feeling full and happy when Sergeant Mackenzie reappeared. 'The High Provost is ready for you now,' he said.

Rather apprehensively, Tom and Sarah got up.

Morag noticed their worried faces. 'Speak up and tell the truth, my dears,' she said kindly. 'He's a fair man. You'll have nothing to fear.'

Sergeant Mackenzie led them upstairs to a high-ceilinged, book-lined study. There, standing before a blazing fire, the High Provost was waiting for them.

He was quite a sight.

To begin with he was huge, a red-headed giant of a

man with bushy eyebrows and a big bushy beard. He was made even more impressive by the fact that he was wearing full Highland dress, with kilt and sporran and ruffled shirt.

Some people look stagey in a kilt, but the High Provost seemed born to it.

Sergeant Mackenzie came to attention by the door. 'These are the young persons I told you of, High Provost.'

The High Provost gave a majestic nod and waved them to two wooden chairs. He sat, facing them, in a massive, high-backed chair, like a kind of throne.

'Your names, if you please?'

'Sarah Martin.'

'Tom Martin.'

'You are brother and sister?'

'Cousins,' said Tom. 'But we were brought up together.'

'I lost my parents as a child,' explained Sarah. 'Tom's parents adopted me.'

'Please accept my sympathy for your loss.' The High Provost paused. 'Now, I would like you to tell me how and why you come to be here.'

'It began when we arrived in London,' said Sarah.

'We went to look for my parents,' said Tom.

The story they told between them was pretty much the truth, although they didn't mention that they'd arrived in a flooded and devastated London from an alternate universe.

They told how they'd visited their old home and found Tom's father's journal and how, with Baz's generous help, they'd set off to find Tom's parents.

The High Provost listened with keen interest.

He was particularly interested in the information Tom had found in his father's journal. He returned to the subject in his questioning, over and over again.

'And you are telling me the truth, now?' he demanded sternly. 'You insist that your parents are scientists? That they were involved in the early transmat experiments and that they still have hopes of perfecting the process?'

'According to the journal,' said Tom. 'That's all we have to go on. We haven't seen them for many years, remember.'

'Did you bring this journal with you?'

Tom shook his head.

'Why not?' asked the High Provost sternly. 'Surely you would not leave a document of such importance to you behind?'

Tom delivered an amended version of the truth. 'We left it in the house – in case some of my parents' friends or colleagues came looking for them.'

When they'd finished, the High Provost said, 'Your story is of particular interest to me. For many years there have been rumours of secret colonies of scientists, somewhere in the far north. Scientists who have preserved some of the knowledge of the past, who have discovered new knowledge – like a perfected transmat device. As you have seen, we have regained a measure of civilisation. We have begun to rebuild. We need these scientists to help us, we need their knowledge.'

'So why don't you ask them to help you?' asked Sarah.

The High Provost spread his big hands. 'Because we cannot find them! These scientists, if they exist, are secretive, suspicious of all established authority – like mine!'

'That's pretty understandable, isn't it?' asked Sarah. 'After the way they were treated . . .'

The High Provost sighed. 'It is, indeed, understandable. As understandable as it is regrettable. As you know, in the early days of the breakdown people turned on scientists, blaming them for all that had gone wrong. Now the scientists have gone underground.' He paused. 'It seems very probable to me that your missing relatives have joined one of these secret colonies. My question is this – did they leave you any precise directions how to find them?'

Before Tom could speak, Sarah said, 'I'm afraid not. We were hoping somebody up here could tell us where they are.'

'You are sure they left no clue?'

'All they said was that they were coming north, and that we should try to find them.'

'And you, young man? You have no further information to offer me?'

Taking his cue from Sarah, Tom shook his head.

'A pity.'

The High Provost rose, towering above them. 'Well, it is growing late. I must ask you to stay the night here, and think the matter over. Perhaps something will come back to you. Morag will show you to your rooms.'

The High Provost rang a little handbell, and a few minutes later, Morag appeared.

'Show these young people to their rooms, please, Morag.'

As they left the room Sergeant Mackenzie said, 'Think over what the High Provost said, the pair of you. If you can help us to find those scientists, you'll be doing us, and them a real service.'

They followed Morag from the room.

She led them up another flight of stairs to two comfortable, old-fashioned bedrooms in the front of the big old house. Night clothes were laid out on each bed.

As soon as Morag had left them, Sarah headed for Tom's room. She found him looking longingly at the bed.

'Looks tempting, doesn't it?' she said. 'Pity you won't be using it!'

'Why not? What's going on, Sarah? Why wouldn't you tell the High Provost that my parents were on Skye? He'd have taken us to find them.'

'That's just it, isn't it? They may not want to be found, not by him. Maybe they've got good reason to distrust authority. What right have we got to give them away?'

'I see what you mean. But what can we do? I think the High Provost is suspicious. He won't let us go until he gets some information out of us.'

Sarah led him to the window and pulled back the long velvet curtain. Down below, still parked in front of the house, was the dusty white Land Rover.

'So we'll go anyway!'

'What about the keys?'

She held out her hand. 'Keys! I palmed them when we parked. Come on, Tom, let's go now before they realise.'

Tom shook his head. 'We can't. We're on parole until midnight. I know it seems daft but I think we should keep our word.' He looked at the expensive, military-style watch he'd acquired on the SS World. 'Meet you on the landing at midnight.'

As the last stroke of twelve died away on some distant grandfather clock, Tom and Sarah crept cautiously down the stairs.

They unbolted the door – luckily the bolts were freshly oiled – and went down the front steps to the Land Rover. They got inside and Tom started the engine and drove quickly down the drive.

Holding back the curtains in his study, the High Provost, a glass of whisky in his other hand, watched the Land Rover disappear. He glanced at the mantelpiece clock.

'Twelve-o-one, precisely. Nice to know the young people have a sense of honour!' He turned to the tall figure beside him. 'Well, here we go, sergeant. Come along!'

'Right you are, sir.' Draining his dram of whisky, Sergeant Mackenzie followed the High Provost from the room.

CHAPTER SIXTEEN

REUNION

IT WAS a tricky drive at the beginning, while it was still dark. But thanks to some efficient navigation by Sarah, and a bit of luck with the signposts, they were well on their way by dawn.

They were driving north west across Scotland, by way of Stirling, Crianlarich and Fort William. The drive took them by steep and winding roads over heather-covered hills.

The towns and villages they passed seemed silent and deserted, though occasionally, as morning wore on, they saw the odd solitary figure trudging along a lane, or working in the fields.

Now and again they saw little groups of sheep or cattle, grazing peacefully on the hillsides.

Sometimes they saw one of the tall semaphore towers, its signal arm waggling to and fro. But no one bothered them, and as far as they could tell, nobody was following them either.

'I think the High Provost must have decided we weren't worth bothering about,' said Sarah.

Tom grinned. 'Not Bonnie and Clyde after all, just a couple of tiresome kids!'

At last, with the sun high in the sky – the skies seemed clearer here in the north – they found themselves at the top of a low hill overlooking a little fishing village, with the blue-grey sea stretching mistily beyond.

Part of the harbour wall had fallen in, and there were one or two wrecked buildings on the shoreline. But there were fishing boats too, bobbing at their moorings. There didn't seem to be anybody about.

'That's it,' said Sarah, checking the map. 'Mallaig. Skye and some other smaller islands are out there somewhere in the mist. How are we going to reach them?'

'We'll have to borrow a boat, I suppose.'

'You mean steal?'

'I mean borrow,' said Tom firmly. 'There's not such a help-yourself policy up here – and we're in quite enough trouble with the law already.'

'Can you handle a boat?'

'Only on the boating lake in the park. How about you?'

'Not even that.'

'Maybe we can hire somebody to take us out there.'

'How are we going to pay them?' asked Sarah. 'We don't know what they use for currency up here – and even if we did, we haven't got any!'

'I know,' said Tom. 'Barter. We'll trade something from

our supplies.'

'Three cans of beans for a boat-ride, you mean?' Sarah laughed. 'I suppose it might work.'

'Well, here's our chance to find out,' said Tom. 'Look, there's a boat coming in from the islands now.'

A small boat had appeared from the mists and was chugging towards the shore.

'Let's go down and ask them,' said Sarah. 'Even if they won't take us, they might know somebody who will.'

Tom started the car and they drove down the hill to the quayside.

The boat was much closer by the time they reached the quayside. It was a simple affair, a kind of outsized rowing boat, propelled by an outboard motor. There were two people on board, a tall, thin man in fisherman's clothes and a woman in a tweed dress with a hooded cloak.

Tom and Sarah got out of the Land Rover and gave them a friendly wave.

The man and woman didn't wave back. They just stared at them, as if they couldn't believe their eyes.

The boat was almost at the shore – and by now Tom and Sarah were staring too.

Sarah clutched Tom's arm. 'Tom, look! Do you see who it is?'

'I know,' said Tom, a little unsteadily. 'Mum and Dad!'

They both ran along the quayside where the man was just mooring the boat, next to a little wooden hut on the quay.

'Mum, Dad!' yelled Tom. 'It's us!'

The woman scrambled out of the boat and ran towards them. Older, greyer, more careworn than they remembered, she was undoubtedly Tom's mother, Sarah's aunt.

She hugged them both to her. 'Tom, Sarah! This is impossible! How *can* you be here?'

The man jumped out of the boat and hurried up to them. He grabbed Tom's hand in a painful grip, and hugged Sarah hard. 'You can't be here!' he said. 'You're supposed to be in Alaska!'

This was going to be the tricky bit, thought Tom. His alternate-world father seemed older, and he looked tough and weathered, not the chairborne academic Tom remembered from their own world. But the keen grey eyes were as shrewd as ever. Peter Martin had never been an easy man to fool.

It was Sarah who came up with some kind of explanation. It wasn't wonderful, but it was better than nothing at all. 'We got worried about you, and decided to come and find you both,' she said.

'But how?' asked Tom's mother. 'How did you possibly manage to get here?'

'We got a relief plane to London.'

'I thought they'd stopped them?' said Tom's father.

'One or two still arrive.'

'Anyway, we went to the house and found your journal and then got hold of a car and drove up here,' said Tom.

He tried to make it sound easy and routine.

His mother wasn't fooled. 'You went to London? It's so dangerous there now!'

'I suppose you decided you couldn't wait for the transmat trials,' said his father.

Tom glanced quickly at Sarah and then turned back to his father. 'You're working on transmat – here?'

His father gave him a baffled look. 'You know we are – it's almost ready. If you'd waited a little longer you might have been able to come by transmat, and avoided all these dangers. Why on earth you didn't wait when we're so close now . . .'

'I don't think we ought to stand here arguing about it,' said Tom's mother. 'It isn't really safe. Let's collect the supplies and go back to the island.'

'Why isn't it safe?' asked Tom. 'Things seem so much better here than in London.'

'They are on the whole,' said his father. 'There's even some kind of local government now, under some colourful chieftain calling himself the High Provost.'

'We've met him,' said Sarah.

'You have?' Tom's father was astonished – and suspicious. 'How? Where? Did you tell him where to find us?'

'Of course not,' said Tom. 'You made it pretty clear you wanted that kept secret.'

'We'll tell you all about it later,' said Sarah.

'The High Provost has been trying to get in touch with

us,' said her aunt. 'But your uncle isn't keen.'

'I don't trust any kind of government any more,' said Peter Martin. 'Look at the way they treated us over transmat! I don't think I trust any non-scientist, come to that. I had too many friends killed in the purges. We're safer on our own.'

'Mum just said it was dangerous here,' said Tom.

'We've been having some trouble with coastal pirates,' said his father impatiently. 'That's what they like to be called, anyway. They're just petty thieves in boats really. They've been raiding the villages around here, and of course they're very keen to find our base. We've got a lot more that's worth stealing than most people.'

'Let's get the supplies and go back to the island,' said Tom's mother. 'We can talk things over there.'

His father looked round. 'I can't understand where old Angus has got to. He's usually very prompt. Maybe he's left the supplies in the hut.'

The hut door suddenly opened and a man stepped out. 'Old Angus has had an accident,' he said.

They all looked at the newcomer in amazement.

He was dirty and unshaven and he was dressed in fisherman's clothes – with the addition of a red bandana handkerchief knotted around his head. There was a knife thrust into his belt and a big revolver in his hand.

He looked both ridiculous and dangerous at the same time.

He really does think he's a pirate! thought Tom.

Three other men followed the first one out of the hut. All three were dirty and scruffy and armed with guns and knives.

'Right,' said the leader. 'Let's go!'

'Go where?' asked Tom's father.

'Out to your island. You're going to take us to the right one.'

'Oh no I'm not!'

'Look,' said the leader wearily. 'Let's not be stupid about this. I've been planning this for some time. I've got you, your wife and your kids. Take us out to that island or I'll kill them all off one by one. You last. Well?'

Peter Martin didn't move or speak.

'We'll start with the girl, then, shall we?'

The leader raised his revolver and aimed it at Sarah.

Tom looked at Sarah, who was standing absolutely still. Then he looked at his father.

Alternate world or not, Peter Martin was still the same man. Somehow Tom knew, just knew, that his father wasn't going to give in. Which meant that they were probably all going to die.

Seemed a shame really, when they'd gone to so much trouble to meet. But at least they could go down fighting . . .

He looked quickly at Sarah and knew she was thinking the same thing. As always at times of crisis, their mental link was hard at work.

Tom was going to jump the man nearest to him. As

soon as Tom moved, Sarah could attack the pirate leader.

Then Dad and Mum could join in.

If just one of them could get their hands on a gun . . .

Tom prepared to spring.

A shot rang out . . .

CHAPTER SEVENTEEN

THE ISLAND

FOR ONE terrible moment, Tom thought that the leader had carried out his threat and that Sarah had been shot.

But it was the leader himself who staggered back, dropping the revolver and clutching at his shoulder.

Tom snatched up the revolver and covered the three men. 'Nobody move!' he shouted.

He heard footsteps behind him, and a familiar voice called, 'All right, laddie, you can leave them to us!'

Tom glanced quickly over his shoulder and saw Sergeant Mackenzie running towards him, a revolver in his hand and a squad of guards at his heels.

'Where did you spring from?' Tom said in astonishment.

The sergeant smiled. 'We were never very far away.'

The guards rounded up the astonished pirates and bustled them away. Two others got the wounded leader to his feet.

'What'll happen to them?' asked Sarah.

Sergeant Mackenzie said, 'We'll take them to Edinburgh, give them a fair trial and then hang them!'

Sarah was about to say something reproachful about the evils of capital punishment when the sergeant added, 'Or since they're pirates, maybe we'll tide them instead.'

'What's tiding?' asked Tom.

'It's a fine old custom for dealing with pirates. You drive a stake into the sands at low tide, tie your pirate to the stake and let three tides wash over him. The High Provost is a great one for keeping up the old traditions!'

'No, please,' begged the pirate leader.

'Of course,' said Sergeant Mackenzie, 'if you could tell us where we might find some of your fellow sea-scum things might go easier on you.'

'Anything,' babbled the leader. 'I'll tell you anything.'

'I thought you might,' said Sergeant Mackenzie. 'All right, lads, take him away. Get that wound seen to, we don't want him dying on us.'

The pirate leader was taken away.

Mackenzie turned to Tom and Sarah. 'Nice to see you again.'

'You followed us!' said Sarah accusingly.

'Let's say we always knew where you were. The watchers in the fields, the semaphore signals . . .'

'And you deliberately let us escape,' said Tom. 'I thought it was all a bit too easy!'

'The High Provost was pretty sure you had a good idea where you were really headed.' Mackenzie turned to the elder Martins, who had been standing silent and astonished all this time. 'I take it this lady and gentleman are your parents?'

'My parents, Sarah's uncle and aunt,' said Tom.

Sergeant Mackenzie nodded politely. 'If they wouldn't mind waiting for a moment, the High Provost would like a word.'

Already the High Provost was striding down the quayside towards them, an impressive figure in a plaid cloak and a Highland bonnet complete with feather.

He nodded politely to Tom and Sarah, but it was Tom's father who really interested him. 'Professor Martin, I presume? I've been hoping to meet you for some time.'

Peter Martin looked hard at him, but made no comment. Instead he said, 'I believe you've already met my son Tom and my niece, Sarah?'

'I have indeed had that pleasure. Two splendidly enterprising young people.'

'You're very kind,' said Peter Martin drily. 'May I present my wife, and my valued colleague, Doctor Helena Martin?'

The High Provost swept off his bonnet in a magnificent bow. 'Charmed, dear lady, charmed!' He kissed her hand.

The social formalities over, he got straight back to business. 'As I say, I've wanted this meeting for some time, Professor Martin.'

'I'm not sure I want it at all,' said Peter Martin bluntly.

The High Provost smiled. 'I understand your suspicion of the civil power, but I want to assure you that my administration is not anti-science. A combination of bad science and man's greed and folly have almost ruined our planet. Now we need good science, responsibly applied, to redress the balance.'

'You need transmat,' said Tom. 'Dad thinks he's got it working properly at last,' he added proudly.

'It will solve all your transport and communication problems,' said Sarah. 'And stop the world getting polluted again. With a transmat network set up, places like this where you're starting to recover can help places like London.'

'Steady,' said Professor Martin. 'It's early days yet.'

'I look forward to hearing the results of your experiments,' said the High Provost politely. 'And to our future collaboration.'

Tom's father hesitated. 'You put me in a very difficult position, sir. I owe you a great deal. My life, and the lives of all my family.'

'A pleasure to be of service. I can promise you that scum won't trouble you again. And may I point out that our collaboration will greatly increase your family's security.'

Professor Martin hesitated. 'To be honest, I'm still not sure how much I want to be involved with the outside world. And of course, I can't speak for my colleagues . . .'

'Let me make you a proposition, Professor Martin,' said the High Provost. 'I won't even ask you for the location of your island base. All I ask is that, some time in the near future, you, and your good lady of course, will come to Edinburgh and discuss the possibility of our future collaboration. I think we could work together.'

The two men studied each other for a moment.

Tom's father held out his hand. 'So do I.'

They shook hands.

'I'll establish a semaphore station here in the harbour,' said the High Provost. 'See to it, will you, sergeant? Send a message when you are ready, professor, and a suitable escort will be provided.'

He swept off his bonnet in another splendid bow and strode away.

'My men have loaded your supplies in the boat for you,' said Sergeant Mackenzie.

'Angus!' said Tom's mother. 'What happened to poor old Angus?'

'We found an old fellow in the hut with the supplies,' said Mackenzie. 'He'd been knocked on the head and tied up, but he'll be fine in a while.'

'You'll look after him?'

'He's on his way to the hospital now. We'll bring him back home when he's better and we'll see he's paid for the supplies. In future, if you'll just give a list of your needs to our man in the harbour here, professor, everything you need will be provided.'

'Looks as if you're back in solid with the establishment, Dad,' said Tom.

Sergeant Mackenzie nodded to Tom and Sarah. 'We'll take care of the Land Rover for you, just ask when you want it. I'll be seeing you again. Stay out of trouble!'

Sergeant Mackenzie saluted and strode away.

A few minutes later they were chugging across the sea towards the island.

'How do you come to have a scientific base right out here?' asked Sarah.

Peter Martin gave her a puzzled frown. 'Surely you both know all this already?'

'It's all a bit complicated,' said Tom. 'We'll explain later, if we may.'

Which won't be easy, thought Sarah. How do you set about explaining you came from an alternative universe? Still, at least they're both scientists, maybe they'll believe us!

'Well, as you know, the base was set up many years ago,' said Professor Martin. 'We needed a place where the air was exceptionally pure for anti-pollution experiments. When all the climate troubles began and the world started to turn against science and scientists, just after you went away, a group of us started to build the place up as a general research centre. There are others like it, hidden all over the country. All over the world.' He sighed. 'I think the idea was that one day we'd emerge and set the world to rights. A ruling scientific élite! But the time never seemed right and we became more and more secretive and reclusive. Perhaps it's time for that to change . . .'

'I think you can trust the High Provost,' said Tom.

'That's right,' said Sarah. 'You need each other . . .'

The base was an extraordinary place. It wasn't actually on Skye itself, but on one of the smaller islands, an island so small that it didn't even have a name. Over the years of the troubles the few surface buildings had been camouflaged. The rock of the island had been hollowed out, and the research laboratories were now all underground.

They landed at a hidden harbour, reached by a tunnel leading into the rock. They went up stone steps, through an automatic door, and found themselves in a different world.

It was a world of air-conditioned, neon-lit corridors. These honeycombed the solid rock, with room upon room leading off.

'We've got everything here,' said Tom's father. 'Laboratories, living quarters, recreation areas, everything powered by our own atomic generator. I'd show you around, but I want to check up on things in the transmat lab. We're expecting a signal from Anchorage – where you've just come from!'

Tom and Sarah looked at each other. 'Can we come too?' asked Tom.

'We've got a special interest in transmat,' said Sarah.

'By all means,' said Professor Martin, already preoccupied by his work. He and his wife hurried through the endless corridors, Tom and Sarah close behind.

They ended up in a huge, brightly-lit laboratory.

White-coated assistants scurried to and fro and the rock walls were lined with masses of complicated electronic equipment.

But it was the cubicle in the middle of the laboratory that drew Tom and Sarah's fascinated attention.

It was a transmat booth.

Still crude and primitive, but undoubtedly the same kind of transmat booth that had once formed such a familiar part of their lives.

An excited laboratory assistant hurried up. 'You're back just in time, Professor Martin. We've had a signal from Anchorage. They're just about to attempt a live transmission! Everything's ready . . .'

Suddenly the cubicle lit up. Everyone waited tensely.

Then slowly, two figures appeared in the booth. A young man and a young woman.

The scientists watched in awed fascination but none of them were as fascinated as Tom and Sarah.

They were looking at themselves. Older-looking, but undoubtedly themselves.

The real, this-world Tom and Sarah had arrived . . .

CHAPTER EIGHTEEN

DEPARTURE

IT WAS quite a moment for all the assembled scientists.

They were witnessing the wonder of the first successful transmat experiment involving human beings.

For Peter and Helena Martin, there was the added complication that the experiment had somehow duplicated two members of their family.

Tom and Sarah had other things on their mind. Once again, those two minds were working as one.

There was no question of staying. Mere closeness to their this-world selves would be enough to bounce them on to another universe.

But since there was a transmat cubicle here, even if it was a new and experimental one, perhaps they could exercise more control over their departure – and their destination.

The newly arrived Tom and Sarah opened the transparent doors of the booth and stepped, beaming, from the cubicle. 'Mom! Dad!' Tom heard his other self cry. 'We made it!'

Mom?

Thoroughly Americanised, thought Tom.

Looking around at the faces of the assembled scientists, the new Tom and Sarah saw not welcome and jubilation but consternation.

Then their eyes fell on their other selves – and they too looked equally astounded.

Professor Martin stared from one set of Tom and Sarah to the other. 'What the devil . . . ?'

'Please, sir,' said Tom urgently. 'I can explain everything. Can we talk to you and your wife – alone?'

After a moment, Professor Martin nodded. He turned to the newly-arrived Tom and Sarah. 'Tom, Sarah, don't panic, we'll sort this out. It's wonderful to see you both again, and congratulations on a brilliantly successful experiment. If you'll give us just a little time to deal with this . . . crisis, we'll be able to talk properly. My colleagues will look after you meanwhile. Now, will everyone please clear the laboratory?'

Puzzled and alarmed but obedient, the little group of scientists ushered the this-world Tom and Sarah from the laboratory.

Once they'd all gone, Sarah said, 'Before you ask, those two are your real son and your real niece, safely arrived by transmat from Anchorage, Alaska. Congratulations!'

Helena Martin said, 'But if they're Tom and Sarah – who are you?'

'We're a sort of alternative version,' said Tom.

Speaking quickly and urgently, Tom and Sarah took it in turns to explain how a transmat malfunction in their own world had sent them to one alternative universe after another – ending up here.

When they'd finished, Professor Martin was silent for a moment, taking it all in.

Then he said, 'It's an incredible story, but not an impossible one. I'm familiar with the alternate-universe theory, so what you're telling us could be true . . .'

'Of course it's true,' interrupted Helena Martin. 'How can you disbelieve the evidence of your own eyes? These two are our son and our niece – and yet they're not. I sensed something strange as soon as we met them. Just as I sensed that the two who just arrived are really the Tom and Sarah we know.'

Professor Martin nodded. 'Then if it is true – what on earth do we do about it?'

'Help us to get home,' said Sarah.

'But how?'

'By transmat,' said Tom. 'We can't stay in this universe with our other selves. If we try we'll just vanish. Let us leave by transmat, now. If we punch in the coordinates for Trafalgar Square in our own world . . .'

'But those coordinates would only apply to a developed system in your own alternative universe,' said Professor Martin. 'They can't possibly work from here.'

'I think there's just a chance that they can,' said Sarah.

'We seem to be linked to transmat in some way. Once we're between the dimensions, the correct coordinates might just lock on.'

Helena Martin said, 'But it's too dangerous. This is only the first time transmat has worked between two different countries. To expect it to work between alternate universes . . .'

'Please, it's our only chance,' said Tom. 'We'll vanish anyway, as soon as we have any contact with our other selves.'

Professor Martin frowned. 'Vanish? Why?'

'I don't know,' said Tom desperately. 'For some reason, that's the way it works. We'll vanish and arrive who knows where. As Sarah says, this way there's a chance of getting home, however small.'

'Please let us try,' said Sarah. 'You've got your family now. We want to find ours.'

Professor Martin and his wife looked at each other briefly, in a moment of silent communication. Then Helena Martin said, 'We've got to let them try, Peter. What else can we do?'

'Very well,' said Professor Martin. 'I'll charge up the transmat booth.'

He went to a nearby control console. Moments later the booth lit up, humming with power.

Tom and Sarah went over to the booth.

'Goodbye,' said Professor Martin.

'Goodbye,' said Helena Martin. 'Good luck.'

'Goodbye,' said Sarah. 'And thank you.'

Tom looked at his alternative-world parents. He wondered if he'd ever see the real ones again. In this world, at least, his family was reunited.

'Goodbye,' he said. 'Give our love to Tom and Sarah!'

They stepped into the transmat booth and the doors closed behind them.

'Quick, coordinates, Sarah!' said Tom.

Sarah punched in the coordinates she'd used back in New York when things first went so disastrously wrong.

Like Tom, she hoped desperately that *somehow* the complex, multi-dimensional web of transmat would pick them up and deposit them at the right destination.

Not a world ruled by SS tyranny, or a ruined, flooded planet, but Trafalgar Square – the Trafalgar Square of their own safe, happy, prosperous, transmat-linked world of 2015.

Before the eyes of their alternative-world parents, Tom and Sarah faded away.

Tom and Sarah stood together in the darkened transmat booth, holding hands, experiencing that strange sense of disorientation that always came with travel by transmat.

Usually it lasted for just a few seconds and you were there. This time it seemed to go on and on . . .

'What's happening, Sarah?' whispered Tom. 'Transmat's supposed to be instantaneous.'

Sarah shrugged. 'Search me! Maybe it's because we

started off in a primitive transmat system.'

'Seems to be going on for ever,' muttered Tom. 'Maybe it will go on for ever!' he said in sudden panic. 'Maybe we're trapped on a permanent transmat trip!'

'Relax,' said Sarah. 'We're arriving, I can feel it!'

Tom could feel it too. Slowly the weird disorientation effect faded away and the booth lit up.

Glancing quickly around, Tom could see that it wasn't the booth they'd set off in. That had been new and experimental, almost unused.

This one was bigger, more solid, and it looked old and battered.

They opened the door, stepped out and looked around them.

'Where are we?' whispered Sarah.

'Well,' said Tom, after a moment. 'It's certainly not Trafalgar Square!'

The booth they'd emerged from was one of a long row.

The row of transmat booths stood in a huge dusty area, bounded by metallic walls but open to the sky.

The air felt hot and dry and hard to breathe, all at the same time.

On the far side of the area was a long counter divided into sections, with queues of shabby, tired-looking people before each section.

Some kind of reception area.

Sarah pointed. 'Tom, look!'

Hanging above the reception counter was an enormous

banner. It was wrinkled and faded as if it had been up there for a very long time.

The banner read:

WELCOME TO MARS

Suddenly a man in a black uniform appeared, hurrying down the corridor towards them. He had heavy, brutal features and he had a holstered pistol at his belt. He was a sinister, frightening figure and Sarah saw that Tom was staring at him in horrified disbelief.

'Oh no!' he whispered. 'It can't be . . .'

'Can't be what?'

'SS,' muttered Tom.

The year is 2015, and the transporter has malfunctioned, reassembling Tom and Sarah in a parallel universe – one in which the Nazis have won World War II. It's a world of soldiers, guns and salutes, of work-camps and swift executions. On the run from the SS and unable to trust anyone, they must try to find a way back to their own universe . . .

"The action is satisfyingly frantic . . . (readers) will respond to Dicks' punchy style and relish the neat twist teasingly placed at the very end of the novel." Books for Keeps

If you would like more information about books available from Piccadilly Press and how to order them, please contact us at:

Piccadilly Press Ltd.
5 Castle Road
London
NW1 8PR

Tel: 0171 267 4492
Fax: 0171 267 4493